EGYPTIAN MAGIC...

As she tipped up her head and the moonlight played on her face, she felt Kane draw nearer to her.

"It is...lovely!" she murmured, "so unbelievably lovely that I...feel it cannot be real...and yet in my heart I know it is!"

"That is what I feel too," he said in a deep voice.

He put his arms around her as he spoke.

Then as Octavia turned to look at him in surprise his lips came down on hers.

It was not what she expected, not what she had even thought might happen.

Yet as he held her close to him and her lips were soft beneath his, it was part of the beauty of the sunset, the mysteriousness of the Pyramids and the feeling of light that came from the Sphinx.

MOONLIGHT ON THE SPHINX

A Camfield Novel of Love

Camfield Place,
Hatfield
Hertfordshire,
England

Dearest Reader,

Camfield Novels of Love mark a very exciting era of my books with Jove. They already have nearly two hundred of my books which they have had ever since they became my first publisher in America. Now all my original paperback romances in the future will be published by them.

As you already know, Camfield Place in Hertfordshire is my home, which originally existed in 1275, but was rebuilt in 1867 by the grandfather of Beatrix Potter.

It was here in this lovely house, with the best view of the county, that she wrote *The Tale of Peter Rabbit*. Mr. McGregor's garden is exactly as she described it. The door in the wall that the fat little rabbit could not squeeze underneath and the goldfish pool where the white cat sat twitching its tail are still there.

I had Camfield Place blessed when I came here in 1950 and was so happy with my husband until he died, and now with my children and grandchildren, that I know the atmosphere is filled with love and we have all been very lucky.

It is easy here to write of love and I know you will enjoy the Camfield Novels of Love. Their plots are definitely exciting and the covers very romantic. They come to you, like all my books, with love.

Bless you,

Books by Barbara Cartland

THE ADVENTURER
AGAIN THIS RAPTURE
ARMOUR AGAINST
LOVE
THE AUDACIOUS
ADVENTURESS
BARBARA CARTLAND'S
BOOK OF BEAUTY
AND HEALTH
THE BITTER WINDS OF
LOVE
BLUE HEATHER
BROKEN BARRIERS
THE CAPTIVE HEART
THE COIN OF LOVE
THE COMPLACENT WIFE
COUNT THE STARS
CUPID RIDES PILLION
DANCE ON MY HEART
DESIRE OF THE HEART
DESPERATE DEFIANCE
THE DREAM WITHIN
A DUEL OF HEARTS
ELIZABETH EMPRESS OF
AUSTRIA
ELIZABETHAN LOVER
THE ENCHANTED
MOMENT
THE ENCHANTED
WALTZ
THE ENCHANTING EVIL
ESCAPE FROM PASSION
FOR ALL ETERNITY
A GHOST IN MONTE
CARLO
THE GOLDEN GONDOLA
A HALO FOR THE DEVIL
A HAZARD OF HEARTS
A HEART IS BROKEN
THE HEART OF THE
CLAN
THE HIDDEN EVIL
THE HIDDEN HEART
THE HORIZONS OF LOVE
AN INNOCENT IN
MAYFAIR

IN THE ARMS OF LOVE
THE IRRESISTIBLE BUCK
JOSEPHINE EMPRESS OF
FRANCE
THE KISS OF PARIS
THE KISS OF THE DEVIL
A KISS OF SILK
THE KNAVE OF HEARTS
THE LEAPING FLAME
A LIGHT TO THE HEART
LIGHTS OF LOVE
THE LITTLE PRETENDER
LOST ENCHANTMENT
LOST LOVE
LOVE AND LINDA
LOVE AT FORTY
LOVE FORBIDDEN
LOVE HOLDS THE
CARDS
LOVE IN HIDING
LOVE IN PITY
LOVE IS AN EAGLE
LOVE IS CONTRABAND
LOVE IS DANGEROUS
LOVE IS MINE
LOVE IS THE ENEMY
LOVE ME FOREVER
LOVE ON THE RUN
LOVE TO THE RESCUE
LOVE UNDER FIRE
THE MAGIC OF HONEY
MESSENGER OF LOVE
METTERNICH: THE
PASSIONATE
DIPLOMAT
MONEY, MAGIC AND
MARRIAGE
NO HEART IS FREE
THE ODIOUS DUKE
OPEN WINGS
OUT OF REACH
THE PASSIONATE
PILGRIM
THE PRETTY
HORSEBREAKERS
THE PRICE IS LOVE

A RAINBOW TO HEAVEN
THE RELUCTANT BRIDE
THE RUNAWAY HEART
THE SCANDALOUS LIFE
OF KING CAROL
THE SECRET FEAR
THE SMUGGLED HEART
A SONG OF LOVE
STARS IN MY HEART
STOLEN HALO
SWEET ADVENTURE
SWEET ENCHANTRESS
SWEET PUNISHMENT
THEFT OF A HEART
THE THIEF OF LOVE
THIS TIME IT'S LOVE
TOUCH A STAR
TOWARDS THE STARS
THE UNKNOWN HEART
THE UNPREDICTABLE
BRIDE
A VIRGIN IN PARIS
WE DANCED ALL NIGHT
WHERE IS LOVE?
THE WINGS OF ECSTASY
THE WINGS OF LOVE
WINGS ON MY HEART
WOMAN, THE ENIGMA

CAMFIELD NOVELS OF LOVE

THE POOR GOVERNESS
WINGED VICTORY
LUCKY IN LOVE
LOVE AND THE MARQUIS
A MIRACLE IN MUSIC
LIGHT OF THE GODS
BRIDE TO A BRIGAND
LOVE COMES WEST
A WITCH'S SPELL
SECRETS
THE STORMS OF LOVE
MOONLIGHT ON THE
SPHINX

A NEW CAMFIELD NOVEL OF LOVE BY

BARBARA CARTLAND

Moonlight on the Sphinx

A JOVE BOOK

MOONLIGHT ON THE SPHINX

A Jove Book/published by arrangement with
the author

PRINTING HISTORY
Jove edition/August 1984

ISBN: 0-515-07732-1

Jove books are published by The Berkley Publishing Group, Inc.
200 Madison Avenue, New York, N.Y. 10016.
The words "A JOVE BOOK" and the "J" with sunburst
are trademarks belonging to Jove Publications, Inc.

PRINTED IN THE UNITED STATES OF AMERICA

Author's Note

After the revolt of Arabi Pasha in 1882, he was imprisoned by Ceylon and did not return to Egypt until 1901. He died in 1911 and is now a National Hero.

When Arabi Pasha had been defeated by the British, Government in Egypt was found to be chaotic. The personal authority of the Khedive was almost nonexistent, the country was on its way to bankruptcy, conditions in the prisons were appalling, landlords could not make their tenants pay rent and the Government had to borrow from a religious fund to pay official salaries.

Lord Cromer was brought from India 'to cope' and with a formidable team of Britons, ran Egypt. High on Saladin's Citadel, above the glorious minarets of the old city, flew the Union Flag while the screwdown guns of the British Garrison commanded Cairo.

Needless to say there were ceaseless intrigues, plots, revolutions and political crisis after crisis but Cromer not only 'coped,' he became in practise the absolute ruler of Egypt.

Great imaginative proposals were launched, the Aswan Dam began, Egyptian Courts were reformed, forced labour was abolished, the railways were re-built, the Army disciplined. Cromer was known simply and truthfully as 'The Lord.'

chapter one

1896

A MAN swung himself off the flat roof and down the drain-pipe, hoping as he did so that it was strong enough to hold him.

He was aware as he slid down that people in the street below were beginning to stare.

There were not many of them as it was only a small side street, but at the same time there were the inevitable layabouts to be found in every port in the world and especially in Alexandria.

They had nothing to do but somehow make a living by picking the pockets of the tourists or carrying pieces of information from one Egyptian to another.

The Egyptians were insatiably curious, and the man sliding down the drain-pipe was aware that what he was doing would be reported in a very few minutes to somebody at the front of the Hotel.

1

He looked for an open window, found one, and with a deftness which could only have come from long practice slipped inside.

He found himself in a bathroom and locked the window behind him.

Then with a speed which sprang from quick thinking rather than from fear he first turned on the water in the bath, then took off his clothes and hid them behind it.

It was one of the deep baths of the kind introduced by the British wherever they went.

It stood on four legs with a curved bottom, so that although it was against the wall there was room for him to slip his clothes behind it and ensure, if they did not touch the floor, they were unlikely to be spotted by anybody bending down to look under the bath.

Quickly he glanced around and saw a pile of clean towels on a shelf.

Then he saw with an expression of satisfaction that hanging on a hook on the door there was a long robe made of white Turkish towelling.

This again was an innovation which the British had introduced to the better class Hotels in Egypt, and he knew it was exactly what he wanted.

There was no time for a full bath, although after what he had been doing he longed for the coolness of it on his body.

Instead he just had time to stand in it to wet his feet, to wash his hands which were dirty from the drain-pipe, then dry them on one of the clean towels which he then deliberately threw on the floor.

Putting on the towelling robe he fastened it around his waist, ran his fingers through his dark hair so that

2

it would look somewhat untidy, and opened the door of the bathroom.

Outside there was a long corridor stretching almost the length of the Hotel.

At the far end he saw two men emerge from where he suspected there was a staircase.

He slipped back into the bathroom, watching them as they talked to a servant who was coming from one of the rooms with a tray in his hand.

Although he could not hear what they said, he could see they were persuading the man to use his pass-key to open a door on the side of the building where he was now standing.

As soon as they were inside the room he looked in the other direction.

As he did so the door opposite him opened and a waiter came out carrying the remains of somebody's breakfast on a tray, and beyond him he had a quick glimpse of a woman with fair hair sitting up in bed looking at a newspaper.

Without hesitation he walked across the passage from the bathroom and as the waiter was turning to shut the door of the room from which he had just emerged, the man was at his side.

"Pardon, Sir!" the waiter said.

"Bring me up two poached eggs, some coffee, rolls, butter and marmalade!"

"Very good, Sir!"

The man walked into the bedroom and as the waiter shut the door quietly behind him, he found himself looking into two large and very frightened eyes.

*　　*　　*

Octavia Birke had, in fact, been thinking as she finished everything on her breakfast tray that perhaps she would not be so hungry later in the day and could therefore manage without luncheon.

Then as she realised she had no idea where she would be, she felt herself tremble and wondered frantically what she should do.

It seemed as if a century had passed since she had left England, and yet it was only a little over a week since Tony had come into her bedroom at the Priory to wake her up.

She was sleeping deeply, exhausted by the time she had gone to bed after looking after her father, besides attempting to keep some of the house clean and cook a meal for Tony, who had arrived from London that night.

He had been in a bad humour, which was not surprising considering the circumstances.

She had done her best to make the meal palatable and had luckily found in the cellar a forgotten bottle of claret, which had pleased him.

He had talked, but Octavia had felt almost too tired to listen, and when the meal was over and she was stacking the plates preparatory to carrying them into the kitchen, he had said:

"There is a great deal I want to say to you, but I can see how tired you are. Go to bed."

"But . . . Papa . . ." she murmured.

"I will sleep in his room tonight," Tony had replied. "If he wakes, which I think unlikely, I will call you."

"You promise to do that? He has not moved all day. But when the Doctor came he thought there was just a chance that he would become conscious again."

4

She knew from the expression on her brother's face that he was hoping that would not happen, and she said quickly:

"I am desperately tired. After what you told me I did not dare to employ any one other than old Mrs. Coles to help in the house."

She thought as she spoke that Mrs. Coles was really no help at all, but she was cheaper than anybody else in the village and did not expect so many cups of tea and things to eat as the other women did.

Before Tony went to London he had frightened her about their financial position and she was quite certain he had far worse news to tell her now.

Apparently however he was prepared to let it wait until the morning when she was rested, and for that she was grateful.

In fact, her head felt as though it was stuffed with cotton-wool, and her brain simply could not begin to take in the huge amount of her father's debts.

They had to be faced sometime, she was well aware of that. At the same time her whole body was screaming:

"Not now! Not now!"

Looking at her white, exhausted face, her brother put his arm around her shoulders.

"You have been a brick, Octavia, and nobody could have done more," he said affectionately. "Go to bed and I will keep the unpleasant things I have to tell you for the morning."

"Thank you, dearest," Octavia replied. "I really am asleep on my feet!"

She had gone up to her bedroom which was next to her father's and looked in at him.

The evening sun was setting behind the oak trees in the Park and casting a golden glow into the huge bedroom where the heads of the family had slept for generations.

The fourth Lord Birkenhall, lying beneath the heavy carved canopy with its velvet curtains, did not move.

He had had a stroke two weeks earlier and since then had been in what the Doctors called a 'coma.'

He had never moved or opened his eyes, and it was even hard to believe he was breathing.

But he was still alive, and as the Doctor had said rather ponderously:

"Where there is life, there is hope!"

It was difficult for Octavia not to say that if she was honest she hoped her father would die without regaining consciousness.

She knew to say so would undoubtedly shock the Doctor, and instead she merely smiled faintly when he said:

"I wish I could be more help, Miss Birke. It is very hard on you to have to nurse your father and do everything else besides."

"I can manage," Octavia replied.

But when Tony arrived back tonight she had thought that she would have to tell him that things could not go on as they were.

However, whatever they had to say to each other could keep until the morning, and she therefore crept into bed, and as her head touched the pillow she fell asleep.

Now Tony was waking her, and as she felt herself coming back through layers of sleep she tried to see him through half-closed eyes.

She thought it was cruelty not to let her go on sleeping as she longed to do.

"Wake up, Octavia! Wake up!" he was saying.

She opened her eyes and he said quietly:

"Papa is dead!"

For a moment his words did not seem to penetrate Octavia's mind.

Then she sat up.

"Did you say—dead?"

"Yes."

She drew a deep breath and pushed back her hair from her forehead.

"I must...go to him."

"What for?" Tony asked. "There is nothing you can do for him now. He is dead! His heart is not beating, and he has no pulse!"

"Poor Papa," Octavia exclaimed involuntarily.

"On the contrary," Tony said in a different tone of voice, "poor us! And that is why we have to do something about ourselves."

"What do you mean?"

"We are going away now, as soon as you are dressed!"

"Away? I do not...understand what you are... saying."

"Then listen to me," Tony said. "I meant to talk to you about it last night, but you were too tired. Now it is too late to talk. We have to act!"

"I...I still do not...understand."

He was sitting on the side of her bed, and was silent for a moment before he asked:

"Have you any idea of the extent of Papa's debts?"

"I have not wished to think about it."

"Well, I will tell you," Tony said. "He owed over fifty thousand pounds!"

"I do not believe it!"

"It is true! I went to see his Solicitors in London, and they told me the exact amount. As you are well aware, there is no money with which to pay his debts."

"Then what can we do?" Octavia asked in a frightened voice.

"We are going away," Tony said, "and let the Solicitors and the executors of Papa's Will cope with the mess."

"How can we possibly do that?"

Tony settled himself more comfortably before he replied:

"Now listen to me, Octavia! I have been thinking about this, and I have decided the only thing we can do to avoid being involved in the muck-heap Papa has created is to get out of reach of anybody who wants to talk about it or any of his Creditors who are foolish enough to ask if we can pay the bills."

"B–but . . . we cannot do that," Octavia objected.

"Of course we cannot," Tony agreed. "There is nothing for ourselves, let alone anybody else."

Octavia instinctively looked about the room as if she thought the very furniture might be able to help her.

As if she asked the question aloud Tony said:

"You are aware the house is entailed, so although they will make Papa a Bankrupt, they cannot sell that. But they can sell off any parts of the estate that were added during his lifetime, and anything in the house that is not on the list of things which now come to me."

He laughed as he finished speaking but the sound had no humour in it.

"As you and I both know, Papa has sold everything worth having although it was illegal for him to do so, and all I am left with is a few extremely ugly family portraits which would not fetch a few shillings in the sales-room, and furniture that is eaten by woodworm and the upholstery in tatters."

"It was very wrong of Papa to sell those things that should have been yours," Octavia said in a low voice.

"The few things he missed, and there were not many, are going to keep you and me alive for a few months at any rate."

"What do you mean?"

"Only that I have followed Papa's example. I sold the last of the family silver last week and also the china in the Blue Drawing-Room."

She gave a little cry.

"Oh, Tony, how could you? Those were Mama's favourites, which is I think, why Papa spared them."

"As I would have spared them," Tony replied, "but his Creditors would have made quite sure they were sold if they did not steal them!"

Because he saw his sister was upset he put out his hand and laid it on hers.

"We have to eat, you and I," he said quietly, "and more important than that, we have to pay our fares to Alexandria."

"Alexandria? Are you mad?" Octavia asked. "Why on earth should we want to go to Alexandria?"

Tony smiled, and it made him look very attractive, as he did when he was not so worried and upset.

"I have been working out that Virginia will reach

Alexandria in her yacht next week," he explained. "She is travelling to Cairo, and I intend to join her."

Octavia looked at her brother in perplexity.

She was well aware that he was attracted by a very lovely American girl who had appeared in London and made quite a stir in the Social Circles in which Tony moved even though she had never had the chance.

There had been no money for Octavia to have a Social Season, and to be presented at a Drawing-Room, attend Balls, and meet the sort of men her mother, had she been alive, would have wanted her to meet.

But Tony was different. As he had said:

"As long as I have the right sort of clothes I can accept invitations to the right sort of parties and it will not cost me a penny."

For Tony therefore the restrictions which were inevitable because they were so desperately poor had not been so acute as they were for her.

When he came home he had talked incessantly of Virginia Vanderburg, and although Octavia knew that he was attracted by her money, he was also attracted by herself.

But would she as an American heiress with the world at her feet consider marrying a completely penniless young Englishman, however attractive?

That was the question Octavia was asking herself, and as if she had spoken her thoughts aloud her brother said:

"I have a feeling that now I have come into the title things will be different. I think Virginia loves me in her own way, and I know that like every American

10

girl she wants, when she marries, to be the envy of her friends."

He spoke simply and Octavia thought he accepted the situation that love was not enough without either a title or money to go with it.

It was something she thought in her heart was rather degrading.

She had sworn she herself would never marry for anything but the idyllic love she dreamt of and which she thought of secretly when she was alone.

But Tony was different, and she knew that after what they had suffered from her father's extravagances and his wild, unceasing gambling, her brother was absolutely determined to marry a wife who could restore the Priory to its original magnificence and to live in the same way their grandfather had.

She supposed when she thought about it that it was her grandfather's extravagance which had been emulated by her father with such disastrous results.

The third Lord Birkenhall had been a great character.

He was a superb rider and a sportsman who was known the length and breadth of the country, while the parties that had taken place at the Priory had never been forgotten.

"Those were th' days!" the older people in the village said.

Her father had always talked of his childhood as if he had lived in a special Heaven.

There had been Balls, huge Hunt Breakfasts, Meets on the lawn, gambling parties that lasted until dawn, and Steeple-Chases in which every rider wagered thousands of pounds on his own chance of winning.

Because his son had watched all this first as a child, then as a boy, he had taken it for granted that when he inherited he would carry on as his father had done.

But times had changed. Living was now far more expensive and some of the sources from which the third Lord Birkenhall's income came had dried up and disappeared.

But he laughed at everybody who tried to warn or advise him. Confident that his luck would change he gambled for higher and higher stakes until finally a threatening letter had brought on the stroke which had left him unconscious.

Now he was dead, but even so Octavia did not think it was right that they should run away.

"We shall have to wait at least until...after the...Funeral," she said.

"Why?" her brother asked. "Papa will not know if we are there or not, and the only people who are likely to attend will be a crowd of his Creditors wanting to listen to the Will and find out if there is any chance of their recouping even a tenth part of their losses."

His voice was sharp. Then he said more quietly looking at his sister:

"You are not going to face them, Octavia, and neither am I. We are leaving, and before anybody realises what has happened, we shall be far away at sea."

"How can we do...that?" Octavia asked.

"Very easily," Tony answered, "because I have been clever enough to collect together enough money to pay our fares."

"But...what will happen to...Papa?"

"I presume the Doctor will call either tomorrow or the next day, and will see to everything. Only Mrs. Coles, or whatever her name is, will think it strange that you are not about."

"I told her not to come today," Octavia said. "I owe her ten shillings as it is. I did not like to ask you for the money the moment you arrived."

"As it happens I could have given it to you," Tony replied, "but it is all the better she is not here. That gives us more time to get out of reach of everybody. Actually I have no intention of telling anyone where we are going."

"Can we...really do...such a thing?" Octavia asked weakly.

She had always allowed Tony, because he was three years older than she was, to do what he liked without arguing, and had accepted that invariably he knew best.

But this was different, and she felt it must be wrong, even though her father had never been a very good parent, to let him be buried without their being present at his Funeral.

Her mother had been the only person who could make him behave sensibly and curb a little of his wild extravagance.

But her mother had been dead for six years, and it was difficult to remember her father except as a man who would not listen to anything his children said to him.

He was concerned only with enjoying himself in ways which left no room in his life for a young daughter.

Octavia had lived at the Priory while her father

13

spent most of the time in London.

Because there was no one with whom she could gossip, Octavia had no idea of the kind of life he lived in an era in which gentlemen of her father's distinction found that everything was planned to make the days and nights one long merry-go-round of gaiety.

Horses, cards, and the alluring glamour of Theatres and Music-Halls could fill their lives from one dawn to the next.

There were parties, parties, parties and where the acknowledged Beauties of the Social World stopped, the Gaiety Girls with their unsurpassed and glamorous allure took over.

Only Tony knew how much money his father had squandered on women whose beauty, like a magnet, enticed the golden guineas from a man's pocket.

Only Tony knew how much money was lost on horses which did not win races, on cards that did not turn up the right number or on the Roulette-Wheel, which inevitably made money for the Bank and not the punters.

It was Tony who came back to the Priory to see his sister and look despairingly at the roof which needed repairing, the windows where the panes were broken, the ceilings which had collapsed from the damp and floor-boards which crumbled if one did not take care where one was walking.

"How can Papa let this happen?" he would ask despairingly.

When Octavia had no answer he drove back to London to watch his father throwing away more and more money without getting any return except more bills, and adding to the throng of importunate Creditors.

What had been the worst problem was that, because his father had so much charm and was still an extremely handsome man, few people had any idea that it was a genuine 'Rake's Progress.'

In fact, as his son thought, only a man who was slightly unbalanced could behave in such a reckless manner.

Everybody including the Prince of Wales liked and admired Lord Birkenhall.

In the Music-Halls his name featured as a Roué in some of the topical songs, and it was said that even the most fastidious Gaiety Girl would throw over a Duke or a Marquis if Lord Birkenhall asked her to supper.

Now he was dead, and the truth was that there was not even enough money with which to bury him decently.

"Now listen, Octavia," Tony was saying, "because we have very little time."

His sister forced herself to try to understand.

"Pack everything quickly that is worth taking with you, and I do not suppose it is much. I will do the same, and when you are ready I will go to the Farm and ask Jake if he will drive us to the station."

Octavia knew that this was what normally happened when Tony was returning to London, and neither Jake, the Farmer's son, nor his father would think it strange.

She wanted to argue with her brother and persuade him that it would be wrong for them to leave.

15

Yet she knew he was right in predicting that once it was known that her father was dead his Creditors would descend on them and the row that would ensue would be very unpleasant.

There would also be a number of relations, who would make things even worse rather than better.

They would all be shocked by the revelation of the reckless way her father had behaved and would be delighted to say now: "I told you so!" and make Tony and herself suffer even more than they were doing already.

Her father had never liked his relatives and had made that quite clear. Only because he was dead would they feel now they could crow over him.

"I cannot watch that happen!" Octavia told herself.

Her brother had risen to his feet.

"Be as quick as you can," he said, "and remember anything left behind will be put in the sale if there is one, or else stolen."

His words made Octavia pack everything she owned although it was in fact very little.

It had been impossible to buy new gowns with the pittance her father gave her when he came home, which was very seldom.

Sometimes she would send frantic letters to London begging for some money for her Governess, the servants, the men who worked in the garden, and the old groom who looked after the few horses that were left.

Then, if she was lucky, she would receive a few guineas. But it was never enough, and gradually the people who had served them either left if they were young, or died if they were old and Octavia was alone.

At first she could hardly believe it was happening

and kept thinking that when her father next came home she would make him understand how difficult it was and things would change.

But things never did change, and when her father did come back eventually she had realised it was because he himself had come to the end of the money he could borrow from friends or Usurers.

He had been forced to leave the world in which he had reigned as a Roué and a spendthrift.

At first he had just mooned about the house, and she suspected he was looking for things he might sell.

Then he systematically drank everything that was in the cellar.

There was one thing Octavia knew her father had never been and that was a drunkard.

He enjoyed good wine as he enjoyed good food, but he had never drunk to excess until, as if it was the only way to escape from the problems that confronted him, he tried to make himself forget them.

It was perhaps that, she thought now, which had brought on the stroke even more than the letter which had made him rage with fury.

He had gone crimson in the face, he had sworn as she had very seldom heard him do before, and then with a strange gurgling sound in his throat he had fallen backwards and never moved again.

Tony was staying at the Priory at the time, and with the help of everybody available they had got him up the stairs into his own bed.

He had been seen by the Doctor although there was no possibility of their paying him.

He had spoken consolingly and hopefully, but gone away without doing anything.

Now it was all over.

When Octavia was dressed before she began to pack she went into her father's room.

It was difficult to believe that the quiet still figure in the bed was the man who had laughed at everything and been one of the gayest, besides one of the most handsome men in the whole of London.

It was not her father lying there, Octavia thought, just his empty body, and she had the feeling that he was somewhere else, still laughing, still finding life a tremendous joke so long as he could find money to pay for it.

She knelt down beside the bed and prayed.

She had meant to pray for her father, but somehow her prayers became a plea for protection both for herself and for Tony.

"Look after us, God," she begged. "I do not know what we are...going to do...but we need You to...help us and to...keep us safe."

She felt the tears come into her eyes but they were not for her father. They were for Tony and herself because they were so alone and for the moment she could only think of them both as children.

She had an intense longing for her mother not only as a person but as a consoling, comforting figure who would put her arms around her and hold her safe.

It had often been frightening, feeling so insecure when her father was alive and knowing there was no money to pay for anything.

But even worse was to know now that Tony was taking her away from the Priory and everything that was familiar.

What would happen to her? And what was the world like outside?

She felt fear creeping over her with an insidious, snake-like movement, encircling her, menacing her so that there was no escape.

Yet where could she go, what could she do, except to obey Tony and leave her home with all its memories behind?

For a moment the future was like a long dark corridor down which she was walking without the slightest notion of where she would find herself at the end of it.

Then she promised herself that Tony would look after her and she would not really be afraid with him.

Suddenly she remembered that she was supposed to be praying for her father.

She said another prayer asking God to bring him peace and let him be happy as he had been when her mother was alive.

She did not wish to think of him as she had seen him last, depressed, showing the first signs of old-age and dissipation from the life he had lived.

She wanted to remember him as he had been when she was a child, riding well-bred horses over the highest fences, lifting her onto the saddle when she was quite tiny, and laughing, always laughing.

The sound of it seemed to echo round the rooms in the vast house and to reach out over the lake to the Park to join with the sound of the birds in the wood.

Then he had been so handsome, so authoritative, so self-willed.

"There is no use arguing with Papa, he always gets

his own way," her mother had said once.

And he had got everything he wanted, very nearly to the end.

But now he had left nothing for her or Tony: nothing but debts and the scandal they would cause.

She could understand why Tony wanted to go away, and he explained it to her even more fully when, having caught the Milk-Train very early in the morning they had arrived at Waterloo Station and from there took a cab to catch the Boat-Train to Tilbury.

"It may not be as comfortable as if we took a ship from Southampton," Tony had said, "but it will be much cheaper, and we do not want to spend a penny more than we have to."

Octavia had agreed. She was already worried as to how he had acquired as much money as he had even though he had admitted to selling some things from the Priory.

They were fortunate to have a second-class carriage to themselves, and once they were settled Tony began to talk.

"I decided to take you with me, Octavia," he said, "because I thought it would be unfair to leave you behind."

"It would have been . . . terrifying to face all . . . those people . . . alone."

"That is what I thought," he said, "and also if neither of us is there it will make it very much more difficult for the newspapers to write about us."

"The newspapers?" Octavia questioned.

"Papa was a celebrity in his way," Tony explained. "When I was in London and the rumour got round that he was ill, reporters kept coming up to me and asking what was wrong with him, and if he was likely to die."

"Why should they be so interested?"

"They could make a good story out of it," Tony replied. "Papa never went anywhere without the newspapers writing about him at First Nights, Race-Meetings, Balls and parties, but that was all in the Court Circular."

"What do you think they will say now?" Octavia asked nervously.

"A great deal," Tony replied, "and I do not want you to read it! It would only upset you. At least this way they cannot ask you what you are feeling about your father's death and how many tears you are shedding over it."

He spoke as if the idea both angered and disgusted him. Then he said:

"That is one reason why we have to get away. The second is that we are going to be blamed for Papa's debts, even though he was responsible for them. Nobody likes a loser."

Again Tony was being bitter, and because Octavia knew how upset he was she put her hand on his arm.

"I am sure you will find some way out of all this," she said softly.

"It is going to be difficult unless Virginia agrees to marry me."

"Is there nothing else you can do?"

"There is nothing else I want to do. I love Virginia for herself. She is adorable, and I understand, perhaps better than anybody else, that she would not want to be tied up to a penniless nobody!"

It occurred to Octavia that if she was really in love

with somebody she would marry him whether he had a title or however unimportant he was.

But she supposed wealthy women like Miss Vanderburg who could choose almost any man she wanted, would think her foolish and she had better keep such ideas to herself.

"If Papa had not messed up my life from the moment I left School," Tony said, "I would have gone into the Army. But even in the most unimportant of Regiments one has to have an allowance of some sort, and I never knew whether Papa would give me any money from one week to the next. So being a soldier was out of the question."

"Is there no way you could make some . . . money?" Octavia asked in a small voice.

"How?" Tony asked. "You must not think I have not thought about it, but gentlemen are not supposed to work, and anyway what qualifications have I, except for enjoying myself, as Papa managed to do?"

Octavia sighed.

Then she slipped her hand into her brother's.

"I am sure when you see Miss Vanderburg again she will want to marry you," she said, "and any girl would be very lucky to have you as her husband."

Tony laughed. Then he kissed her cheek.

"What is also important is that we should find you a very rich husband!"

For a moment Octavia thought he was joking, then she realised he was speaking seriously.

"No," she said quickly, "no, I do not want one!"

"Do not be silly, dearest!" Tony replied. "Of course you have to be married. You have no choice, and I have a feeling in Cairo, which is full, I am told, of British soldiers, British tourists, and has adopted a British way of life, you will have a much better choice and with much less competition than in London."

Octavia looked at him wide-eyed and he went on:

"You know I will do my best to look after you, and you are very lovely, Octavia. Dressed properly you will find that dozens of men will fall in love with you!"

Octavia wanted to say that this was a rather frightening prospect but her voice seemed to have died in her throat.

She could only listen and go on listening all the time they were travelling to Tilbury.

Then they went aboard the small, not very clean steamer that was to carry them to Alexandria.

Afterwards, when she thought back over the journey, she realised how unpleasant it had been and tried to erase it from her mind.

Not only was the ship uncomfortable and filled with people whom Tony despised and looked at with disdain, but the sea was extremely rough, and everybody was seasick.

Because Octavia was so worn out from looking after her father and doing everything else at the Priory she was fortunately able to sleep.

Despite the hardness of the bunk in her cabin, the creaking of the ship's timbers, and the smell that came from the engines, she slept almost incessantly until they reached the calm waters of the Mediterranean.

Then the blue of the sea and sky, and the warmth of the sun made her feel it was too much trouble to complain and it became easier to anticipate that once they reached their destination everything would be better.

It was in fact much better, and she was so relieved to step ashore at Alexandria that she was entranced with almost everything she saw and forgot the discomforts which were now over.

Tony had hurried her off to an Hotel, then gone in search of the woman he had come so far to see.

He eventually returned smiling and excited to say that the yacht was in harbour, but Virginia had gone off to explore the sights and would be back by dinner-time.

"I am so glad for you, dearest," Octavia said.

"I expect she has a large party on board," Tony replied. "I will take you to Cairo with me, and I am sure there will be somebody, even if they are Americans, who will see you have a good time."

Octavia knew he was speaking of men and felt a little tremble of fear go through her.

It would not have occurred to Tony that she would be frightened because she had met so few men since she had grown up.

She wondered what she would say to them and if they would find her a bore because she had lived in the country and would know nothing of the things that they were talking about.

Tony was in tremendous good spirits having found Virginia's yacht.

Octavia was sure she was right in thinking that he was really attracted not only by the American girl's money, but also by the girl herself.

At six o'clock when he had been told Virginia was

expected back from her expedition he had returned to the Quay.

"Do not unpack," he said to Octavia. "I am hoping when I return to take you down to the yacht."

She obeyed him, and being too nervous to walk about the Hotel by herself she sat in her bedroom waiting for him to come back.

He did not return however until it was nearly dinner-time.

After he had knocked on her door and she had let him into her room she had seen that he was looking serious.

"What . . . is it?" she asked. "W–what is wrong?"

He had seated himself on the bed beside her and taken her hand in his.

"It is not exactly wrong," he said, "but–you will not like what I have to tell you."

"What is it?" Octavia asked nervously.

"Virginia was delighted to see me," he said, "in fact, I honestly think she missed me, but she has changed her mind about going to Cairo!"

Octavia looked at him wide-eyed.

She knew because Tony was not looking directly at her that he was going to tell her bad news.

"She intends to go to Constantinople," he went on, "because somebody has persuaded her it is a place worth seeing."

"Constantinople!"

"Yes, and although she wants me to go with her, the yacht is so full she says you cannot come too."

Tony spoke in a restrained voice as if he found it hard to tell her what he had to say.

There was silence until Octavia asked:

"Then . . . what am I to . . . do?"

"It is quite easy," Tony said soothingly, "you will just have to go home!"

"Go . . . home?" Octavia repeated stupidly, because for the moment she felt she did not understand.

"There are ships leaving almost every day for London," Tony said, "and all you have to do is to tell the Concierge here in the Hotel to book you a place on one of them. I am leaving with Virginia now. I have to! Oh, Octavia, try to understand that I have to go with her! She wants me to, and if I refuse I may never see her again!"

Tony's fingers had tightened on hers as he spoke.

"Y–yes . . . yes . . . of course you must go!" Octavia said in a voice that did not sound like her own. "I . . . I shall be . . . all right!"

Tony gave a deep sigh which she knew was one of relief.

"I knew you would be a brick about it," he said, "and someday I will repay you, I promise you!"

She knew he was thinking he could do that once he had married Virginia.

"I shall be quite . . . all right," she said again as if to reassure herself.

"Just tell the Concierge to book you a cabin on the next ship," Tony said. "There will be one leaving tomorrow."

He rose from the bed.

"You do understand, dearest? I feel a swine, and I tried—I tried desperately to take you with me, but she said it was impossible to have another woman aboard."

"I will go . . . back . . . to England."

"Perhaps by then the worst will be over," Tony said vaguely, "and I will write and tell you as soon as there is a chance of my seeing you."

"Thank . . . you."

He put his arms around her and kissed her.

"You are wonderful!" he said. "Nobody ever had a better sister than you."

As he spoke he drew his watch from his waist-coat pocket.

"I shall have to hurry!" he said. "Goodbye, dearest!"

He walked towards the door, and as he did so Octavia gave a cry of horror.

"Tony, I have no money!"

"Oh, my God, I almost forgot! I have paid the bill downstairs, and here is enough to get you home."

He took some notes from his wallet and put them down on the bed.

"There is £25," he said, "and I will send you some more as soon as I can spare it."

Octavia did not even look at the money.

She was fighting back the tears that were coming to her eyes and the feeling that she must hold onto him and not let him go.

She was frightened, terribly frightened of being alone.

But before the words could come to her lips, before she could say anything, he smiled at her, opened the door and shut it behind him.

She heard him going into the next room which adjoined hers and had the feeling that he had already sent a servant to collect his trunk.

In fact, she was sure of it when after giving himself

27

just enough time to look around to see if he had forgotten anything she heard him shut the door behind him.

Then there were only his footsteps going quickly down the passage.

She was alone, completely alone.

chapter two

FOR a moment the man in the white Turkish towelling bathrobe stood staring at Octavia.

Then because she was nervous she said in a hesitating little voice:

"I . . . I think you have come to the . . . wrong room!"

"You are English!" the man exclaimed. "Thank God! I thought you must be when I saw the colour of your hair!"

Octavia only stared at him, wondering what she could say or do, while he walked towards the bed and added in a low voice:

"Will you please help me as one English person to another? I am desperate, and I need your help!"

Her first thought was that he was going to ask for money, and she was wondering frantically how she could explain to him that she could not possibly help him when he went on:

"It may sound melodramatic, but it is actually a matter of life and death, and my life at that!"

Octavia thought he must be mad, but he continued:

"In a few minutes two men will come into this room who intend to murder me, but if you will agree to pretend that I am your husband, I may be able to escape."

With a superhuman effort, Octavia managed to gasp:

"I . . . I do not understand . . . I do not know what you are . . . saying!"

"Then please do what I ask you to do," he said, "for if you denounce me as an imposter, I assure you I am not exaggerating when I tell you I shall die!"

He spoke in such a calm manner that she found herself almost against her instinct believing him.

Then he said:

"I think I can hear them coming. Lie down and appear to be half-asleep."

Octavia thought afterwards it was the authoritative way he told her what to do which made her obey him as if it were an order.

At the same time as she wanted to protest and refuse to do what he asked, she found herself sinking back against the pillows and he took the newspaper from her.

A second later there was the sound of a key turning in the lock and with a swift movement the man pulled back the sheet on his side of the bed and got into it.

It was then Octavia felt she must scream, but he was not touching her and as he sat on the edge of the mattress as far away from her as possible, she knew that she was really too frightened to do anything.

He opened the newspaper and as two men came

into the room he looked over the top of it.

They were both very unprepossessing Egyptians, one wearing a fez, the other a European jacket over the traditional loose native trousers.

They stood just inside the door which the waiter with his pass-key had opened on their instructions, and he was now peering apprehensively over their shoulders.

Without hurrying himself the man in the bed lowered the newspaper still further before he asked:

"What is it? What do you want?"

The two men looked round the room as if they suspected that somebody was hiding there, but it was simply furnished and there was nowhere where a man could conceal himself.

Then one of them asked:

"You are English?"

"Yes, we are English," the man in the bed replied, "and I would be interested to know on whose authority you are questioning us or why you should come into our bedroom without knocking."

The men did not speak, but only looked at him, their suspicions very evident in their dark eyes.

As if they suddenly annoyed him the man in the bed went on:

"Now I think of it—it is intolerable, and I shall certainly complain to the Manager!"

He looked towards Octavia as he added:

"My wife is tired, and I have no wish for her to be disturbed. Kindly leave at once!"

The way he spoke and the sharpness of his voice seemed to impress the men more than what he actually said.

31

They looked at each other, and then as if they agreed they had made a mistake the one who had spoken before said:

"My apologies, Sir! We thought there was somebody else in this room."

They did not wait for the man in the bed to reply but turned and walked back into the corridor and the waiter shut the door behind them.

The man in the bed was quite still and as Octavia began to sit up and would have spoken he put his fingers to his lips.

She realised he was listening, and several seconds passed before she heard footsteps receding into the distance and knew the two men had in fact, been standing outside the door.

Only then did the man get out of her bed and tidying the sheet and blanket said:

"I can only thank you from the bottom of my heart! You were magnificent!"

"Would they . . . really have . . . killed you?"

"If I had been alone they would have done so at once. As you and the waiter were there, I should have been taken away 'for questioning,' and undoubtedly would have been found later in the day dead in a dark alley, or floating upside down in the sea."

She gave a little exclamation of horror before she asked:

"Why? What have you . . . done?"

"Nothing criminal, I promise you," he said, "and I want you to believe me, because I still need your help."

Sitting up in bed with her hair falling over her

shoulders, her eyes still wide and frightened, Octavia looked very child-like.

Then the man standing looking at her said in a voice that was suddenly beguiling:

"I know it is a great deal to ask of you, but as I have no wish to take unnecessary risks and as I am quite sure they are still watching me, I cannot retrieve my clothes unless you help me."

"Your...clothes?"

"I climbed into the Hotel through the bathroom window," the man explained, "which was where I was fortunate enough to obtain the robe I am wearing."

Octavia gave a little smile before she said:

"There is usually one in the bathroom opposite."

"Which was very lucky for me," he answered. "I have hidden the clothes I was wearing behind the bath, tucked against the wall so that they cannot be seen unless you actually look for them."

"And you want...me to...fetch them?"

The man sat down on the side of the mattress facing her.

"What I would like you to do, if you would be so kind," he said, "is to go into the bathroom in a few minutes and have a bath just as if it was a normal procedure."

"It would be!" Octavia murmured.

"Then when you come back here," he said, "put my clothes over your arm and cover them with a bath-towel, being certain that anybody watching cannot see you are carrying anything beneath it."

"For how...long will they be...watching?"

The man shrugged his shoulders.

"Time, as I expect you know, is unimportant in the East. They know I entered the Hotel on this floor and when they have searched all the bedrooms and not found me, I hope they will believe I have escaped. But I cannot be sure until I get away unharmed!"

Because it was frightening to think of him being killed, even though he spoke it quite calmly, Octavia gave a little shiver.

Then she said impulsively:

"I will help you, but... suppose I do something wrong... and inadvertently betray you?"

The man smiled and it seemed to transform his face.

"I do not think you will do that. I might have known that with my usual luck I would find somebody like you, and I know you will not betray me!"

"There must be some reason... something you have... done," Octavia said, "to make men like that... wish to... murder you!"

"It is a long story," the man replied, "and as I want to leave as soon as possible, I can only ask if you would be kind enough to help me, and leave explanations until I have more time."

As he spoke there was a knock on the door and they both stiffened.

The man glanced at Octavia—and she realised he was warning her—before he said:

"Come in!"

There was the sound of a pass-key turning in the lock, then the door opened and it was the same waiter who had brought Octavia's breakfast bringing what the man had ordered when he entered the room.

"My breakfast!" he exclaimed. "Good! I am extremely hungry!"

He indicated to the waiter a small round wicker table which stood in the window.

As the waiter placed the tray there the man said to Octavia:

"Have you by any chance any small change, darling?"

"Yes . . . of course," she said quickly.

She looked as she spoke to where her handbag was standing on the dressing-table, and picking it up the man brought it to her.

She opened it, found a few small Egyptian coins in her purse which was the change that Tony had given her after he had paid the carriage that had brought them from the ship.

She handed one of the small coins to the man and he gave it to the waiter, who bowing and saying: "Thank you, Sir, thank you!" left the room.

Only when he had gone did the man say:

"Forgive me for having to borrow money from you, but what I have with me in my pocket is in large notes, and I thought it would be a mistake for the waiter to see it."

"Yes, of course," Octavia agreed.

The man looked at the food on the tray and said:

"As I have not eaten since early yesterday I am extremely hungry. So I am going to suggest that I sit down at the table with my back to you so that you can get up and go into the bathroom without feeling embarrassed."

"Thank you."

Octavia knew as she spoke that he was taking com-

plete command of her. She felt she had no will of her
own but just did exactly what he said as if she was a
puppet and he was pulling the strings.

The man sat down at the table and having filled
the cup with coffee began to eat in a way which told
Octavia he had spoken the truth when he said how
hungry he was.

She slipped out of bed and took down her dressing-
gown which she had unpacked last night and which
was hanging in the wardrobe.

Putting it on she slipped her feet into a pair of worn
slippers.

Then she found her sponge-bag in which she had
packed her sponge, flannel, a cake of soap, her tooth-
brush and a box of tooth-powder, and walked towards
the door.

She felt somehow she should say something, but
the man eating in the window appeared to have forgotten her existence.

After a shy little glance at him she went out of the
room and crossed the passage to the bathroom.

It gave her a creepy feeling to think that somebody
was watching what she did, and they might even be
listening to hear that she turned on the taps.

She ran the bath until it was three-quarters full,
just taking the chill off the water. The air was very
hot and she wanted to cool her skin.

She thought that to lie in a bath would make her
feel more relaxed and less apprehensive.

Then as she did so she thought that this extraordinary situation seemed like something out of a book,
and not in the least real.

How could she have imagined for one moment that

she would find herself involved in some of the desperate dramas which she had heard happened in foreign countries, but had not seemed to have any connection with the English?

Why, she asked herself, was this Englishman being pursued by Egyptians who were obviously not Policemen and who were from their appearance very unpleasant characters?

What had he done?

They obviously had no authority to have rooms opened for them in the Hotel by the servants without permission of the Management.

It all seemed a strange and unaccountable mystery.

She could not help hoping that before he left her the man who had come to her room would tell her a great deal more.

Otherwise she felt her curiosity would remain unsatisfied for the rest of her life with no chance of her ever learning the end of the story.

She lay in her bath but not as long as she usually did, and when she got out she dried herself carefully.

She could see the used towel on the floor of the bathroom and although she took another from the pile that was on the shelf, that still left two more.

Only when she put on her nightgown and her dressing-gown again did she look behind the bath.

When she first inserted her hand she thought that either he had told her a lie, or else his clothes had been removed.

Then as she reached down further she found them and pulled them from their hiding-place.

There was a pair of trousers, a shirt, and a pair of white canvas shoes of the type used by the English for playing Tennis, or perhaps in the heat of Egypt for walking, because they were more comfortable than leather.

She put the shirt and trousers over her arm as he had told her to do, then holding the shoes in her hand she threw a fresh towel over them, making quite certain that nothing was showing beneath it.

At the same time she felt it was a little bulky and was glad when she came from the bathroom there was only a few steps before she reached her own door.

She had not thought to take the key with her and knocked on the door, thinking it seemed more natural if she were really the man's wife that he should open the door to let her in.

He must have been waiting for her, for immediately the door opened and he said in a voice loud enough to be overheard:

"Have you had a nice bath, darling? I am sure you feel cooler now."

When she was inside the room he shut the door and he asked in a different voice:

"I thought you would not fail me. Did you notice anybody about?"

"No, nobody," she answered, "but I thought it would be a mistake to look round as if I expected somebody might be watching me."

"That was very intelligent of you."

He took his clothes from her, and as he did so she saw he had eaten everything, including all the rolls that had been brought for his breakfast, and the two glass dishes which had contained butter and marmalade were both empty.

Then she was suddenly aware that she had left her handbag on the bed.

38

She had never thought of it until this moment.

With an apprehension which seemed almost like a dagger in her heart she wondered if the man of whom she knew nothing had taken the opportunity that she had made so easy for him of stealing the money from it which Tony had given her.

She had a wild desire to seize her bag to look inside it and learn the worst, if that was what she would find.

Then she told herself that if he was a thief it might be a very stupid and perhaps dangerous thing for her to do.

She did not speak, but in some way she did not understand he must have read her thoughts for he said unexpectedly:

"I assure you whatever else I may be, I am not a petty thief, I would never behave in such a dishonourable manner towards somebody who has helped me as you have done."

The way he spoke brought the blood surging into Octavia's cheeks and she replied incoherently:

"I . . . I did not . . . accuse you . . . of doing such a thing."

"No, but you thought it."

"How . . . could you . . . know that?"

"Shall I say that your eyes are very revealing!"

"I am . . . sorry that I should have even thought such a thing," she said, "but all the money I possess in the world is in that bag . . . and I suppose it was very foolish of me not to take it with me."

"Very foolish!" the man agreed. "You should learn never in Egypt, or for that matter any other foreign country, to leave money lying about in your room."

He spoke severely as if he was reproving a child,

and Octavia feeling she must excuse herself said:

"I . . . I have never been . . . abroad before, and everything about it makes me . . . realise how . . . ignorant I am."

"You say all the money you possess is in this bag?" the man asked.

She nodded.

"It does not sound as if it is a great amount," he remarked.

"It is enough to take me home."

"To England?"

"That is where I have to go."

She spoke with a note of despair and he asked:

"And yet you have only just arrived!"

"H–how do you know that?"

"I have been trained to be observant," he replied, "and I can see you have not yet unpacked your trunk, and by the label on it you arrived by ship."

"Yes, we came here . . . yesterday."

"We?"

The monosyllable was sharp.

There was a little pause.

"My . . . brother . . . came with me . . . but he . . . had to leave . . . unexpectedly for . . . Constantinople."

Because Octavia felt embarrassed at explaining why she was alone, and in retrospect Tony's behaviour seemed somehow indefensible, she hesitated over the explanation and did not look at the man as she spoke.

She did not therefore see the look of cynical understanding in his eyes, and was unaware that he did not believe the 'Tony' of whom she spoke was her brother.

"How much money has he left for your journey?"

Because it was a direct question, and because there

seemed no particular point in telling him to mind his own business, Octavia told the truth.

"I have £25," she said. "It is enough?"

He knew from the way she asked the last question that she was worried and actually had no idea what her return ticket to England would cost.

"It all depends upon how you intend to travel," he said, "but I expect it will be enough."

Octavia's eyes opened very wide before she said:

"It must be! And Tony said I was to ask the . . . Concierge to book me a cabin on a ship leaving for England today . . . and when I am . . . dressed I must go . . . downstairs and talk to him."

"I have a better idea that may help you," the man said, "but first I think we should both get dressed."

"Yes . . . of course," Octavia agreed.

Then she blushed because it seemed embarrassing that they should both be wearing night-things.

"As I have no wish to be seen," the man said, "I suggest you take your clothes and go back to the bathroom as if you have forgotten something. When you are there dress, except, if you like, for your gown, and by the time you return I shall be looking more respectable."

It seemed a sensible solution and Octavia smiled as, hoping he was not watching, she picked up her underclothes from the chair where she had placed them the night before.

Her petticoat was hanging up in the wardrobe and she lifted it down, leaving the gown in which she had arrived, and which was really the only decent dress she possessed.

Then putting the towel over the clothes she moved towards the door.

Only as she reached it did the man say:

"You have forgotten something."

"My bag?"

"I told you never to leave it behind you, but always to take it with you in a foreign country."

She was just about to say that she trusted him, when an idea came to her and with a little cry she said:

"You are not going...away while I am in the bathroom? You will be here when I come back?"

"Do you want me to be?"

"Oh, please! There are so many things I want to ask you, and perhaps you could...advise me about...a ship."

She did not know why she asked him such things, but quite suddenly, whatever he had done, however strange he might be, she felt she would rather talk to him than be alone.

Besides, the two Egyptians coming into the room had made her feel afraid not for him but for herself.

It struck her now that to be without anybody to whom she could turn for assistance in the big port of Alexandria was very frightening. Because he at least was English and they spoke the same language she did not wish to lose this stranger.

She thought he looked at her reprovingly before he said:

"I promise you I will be here when you return."

She gave him a smile that made her look even younger than she really was.

"Then guard my bag for me," she said and slipping out of the room ran into the bathroom.

It only took her a few minutes to dress herself up to her petticoat and put over it her dressing-gown.

Then she hurried back to find the man she had left looking different in a way she could not explain.

Now he appeared to have even more authority and to be very much more masculine than he had been before.

As she met his eyes she felt herself blushing.

"You have been quick!" he said. "Again I need your assistance."

"What has . . . happened?"

"Nothing more terrifying than that my shirt looks very much the worse for wear, and I am wondering how I could clean it."

The drain-pipe down which he had slid had obviously been extremely dirty, for while his thin cotton trousers had survived the ordeal, his shirt was stained down the front in a way which Octavia realised might be very revealing to anybody watching for him.

She stared at it for a moment, wondering how long, if she washed it, it would take to dry, when she had a sudden idea.

The day before they docked Tony had come to her cabin with one of his shirts in his hand.

"I have lost two buttons from this shirt," he said.

"Have you got them?" Octavia asked.

He shook his head.

"They must have been lost in the wash."

"Then I cannot sew them back on again, can I?" she said. "We will have to buy some as soon as we get to Alexandria."

"Yes, of course," Tony agreed. "Do not let me forget!"

But she had forgotten in the crisis of his leaving without her.

However at least the shirt was clean and would not

43

attract the attention of those who were trying to murder the man who would be wearing it.

"I think I can solve your problem," she said.

She opened the trunk and found, as she remembered, Tony's shirt was quite near the top.

She pulled it out and as she did so saw her little sewing-bag in which she carried her needles, thread, thimble and scissors.

"I tell you what I will do," she said, "I will cut the buttons off your shirt and sew them onto this one."

She somehow felt he was waiting for an explanation and added:

"My brother gave it to me because two buttons were missing, and I was going to sew them on for him."

Again she was not aware that the man looked sceptical when she spoke of her brother.

Aloud he said:

"I am very grateful to you for once again being an Angel of Deliverance!"

He pulled off his shirt, and because Octavia found it embarrassing that he was naked she did not look at him.

As if he understood what she was feeling, he picked up the towelling robe and threw it over his shoulders.

Then he watched as Octavia cut two buttons off his shirt and sewed them quickly on to Tony's.

As she handed it to him he said:

"As I came away in what might be described as a hurry, I am wondering if by any chance you have something in your trunk which I could use as a tie?"

"Yes, I think I have," Octavia replied.

She looked in the tray on the top of her trunk and found a satin belt of dark green ribbon which she had

44

made for one of her gowns.

She held it out to him and he said:

"That will be perfect, but it may be a little long."

"Then you must of course cut it."

She thought as she spoke that it was a pity to spoil the belt, but it would be niggardly of her to begrudge it if it was instrumental in saving his life.

The man put on the shirt, tucked it into his trousers which had a belt round the waist, then going to the dressing-table tied the tie neatly around his neck.

It was too long, and without speaking Octavia merely held out her scissors to him.

"I will buy you another one," the man said, "but now, put on your gown. I want to talk to you."

As he spoke he moved to the window to stand with his back to the room and she realised he was being tactful.

She lifted her gown down from the wardrobe, put it on, and was aware when she had done so that her hair was still hanging over her shoulders.

Without telling him she was dressed, she sat down at the dressing-table and twisting her hair into a thick coil she arranged it in a knot at the back of her head.

The man who had turned round to watch her, knew that this style was the latest fashion introduced by the American artist Charles Dana Gibson.

He had produced a spate of drawings which had delighted every American girl, and were now spreading to Europe.

As Octavia finished arranging her hair she turned her face towards him saying:

"Now I am ready, and what were you going to tell me?"

She expected he was going to explain the predicament he was in and what had caused it.

Instead he sat down on the side of the bed before he asked:

"Is it important that you should return to England?"

Octavia shook her head.

"No, and I never imagined that the moment I arrived I would have to ... go back."

"Then why do you have to go?"

"I thought you understood. Because I have ... no money and know ... nobody. I cannot stay here alone."

"No, of course not," he agreed, "and that is why I have a proposition to put to you."

It was not what she expected him to say, and she asked:

"What is ... it?"

"Because you are so intelligent, and because you have already helped me, I am prepared, if you are interested, to offer you £20 a week to work for me."

"To ... work for you? But ... how?"

He did not speak and she exclaimed:

"But, £20 is much too much! I could not possibly earn that!"

He laughed.

"That is something you should not say until you know what I want you to do. It is a great mistake in life to under-value yourself."

"I have ... no wish to do that," Octavia said, "but I must be honest with you ... and tell you I have no qualifications, and I therefore cannot see how I can earn anything."

"As I have already said," the man replied, "you are intelligent, quick-witted, and certainly somebody who can be trusted in an emergency."

Octavia gave a little laugh.

"Thank you for saying all those nice things to me, but I feel they are not worth very much in hard cash."

"They are to me!"

She looked at him as if she could hardly believe he was serious before she said:

"Are you . . . really offering me so much money to . . . work for you?"

"I am!"

"But . . . you have not told me what you expect me to do. If you are asking me to be your secretary . . . I must tell you I cannot use a typewriter, I am very bad at arithmetic, and not very good at spelling!"

He laughed again.

"You are devastatingly honest, which is a mistake if you want a job. You should always convince the person who is employing you that you are indispensable."

"How can I do that unless I tell a lot of lies which would be discovered the first day I went to work?"

"It depends what the work is."

"Then please tell me how I can work for you."

"Is that something you would like to do?"

"Anything would be better than having to go back to England!" Octavia said quickly.

She paused.

"That sounds rude," she added, "and I do not mean it . . . like that. It is just that there are . . . things in England which I should have to . . . face that would be almost as . . . frightening as being . . . here alone."

She was thinking as she spoke that without Tony supporting her, to be confronted by her father's angry Creditors and the disagreeableness of her relatives would be horrifying.

"If you feel like that about it, it would be quite

easy for you to agree to what I have to suggest!"

"Tell me what it is."

He smiled.

"First, after all that has happened already, I think we should introduce ourselves. What is your name?"

"Octavia Birke."

As she spoke Octavia thought that she had made a mistake and perhaps she would have been wiser to give him a false name.

Then she knew there was no reason why he should suspect that she was anybody of importance or that her father had a title.

He would obviously assume that no well-brought-up young Lady would be alone in an Hotel in Alexandria.

"I like Octavia," the man remarked, "and it is a name I have not come across before."

"I was Christened after my grandmother, and I have always thought it unfair to be saddled with a name which always seems to surprise everybody who hears it."

"It is as unique as you are yourself."

She felt for a moment he was paying her a compliment.

Then as he spoke in a dry, impersonal tone she felt he must be referring to the circumstances in which he had found her, rather than to herself.

"My name," he said, "is Kane Gordon!"

Octavia gave a little laugh.

"Kane is as unusual a name as mine!"

"It is Celtic, as it happens," he replied, "and just as you were Christened after one of your relatives, so was I."

"That makes at least one bond we have in common."

"I think there are already several others," Kane said. "Now I want you to listen to me very carefully."

"Yes . . . of course."

She turned the chair round on which she was sitting in front of the dressing-table so that she was facing him, while he sat on the bed.

"What I am going to ask you," Kane said, "is whether you are prepared to help me as you have done already, by continuing to be my 'wife' until I have left Alexandria and reached Cairo."

Octavia's eyes widened, but she did not speak as he went on:

"When we get there it may be safe for you to work for me in a different capacity, but I cannot be certain what that will be until I am at least free from being pursued by the men you have just seen."

"Do you think they still suspect you are the man for whom they are searching?"

"I wish I knew the answer to that question," Kane replied, "but I am quite certain they will watch me, or rather us, until we leave Alexandria. Then they may either look elsewhere or continue to shadow me."

"You have not yet told me . . . why they wish to . . . kill you."

"That, as I have already said, is a long story," Kane answered. "What I want to do, if you agree, is to leave here immediately and take the first train available to Cairo. There, if we are not followed, we shall have time to breathe and make plans for the future."

Octavia drew in her breath.

"And you . . . really want me to . . . come?"

"Shall I say that you are my mascot? And if you are with me, I shall be at least 50 percent safer than if I leave here alone."

"Then of course I will come with you."

"Do you really mean that?"

"I would like to be able to help you, and please . . . you need not . . . pay me as much as you have . . . offered."

"What I pay you is immaterial when viewed in the light of how exceedingly brave you have been, and I am very grateful."

"You have saved me from having to go . . . straight back to England," Octavia said in a low voice.

She was quite certain that Tony would strongly disapprove of what she was doing. But, after all, it was his fault that she was alone and involved in this strange, and rather frightening drama which she did not understand, but which might have resulted in an Englishman being killed.

"I am very honoured, Octavia, that you trust me," Kane was saying.

It was true, Octavia told herself. She did trust him.

There was something about him which seemed completely and absolutely trustworthy, even though prudence told her she should ask him a thousand more questions before she agreed to anything.

He stood up.

"Now we are both ready to check out of the Hotel," he said, "and I want you to come downstairs with me while I send a Porter up to collect your trunk."

Octavia looked at him.

"I have an idea," she said, "and I hope you will not think it impertinent of me."

"You could not say anything to me that I would consider impertinent," Kane replied firmly.

"I think ... as you said we are travelling by train to Cairo ... you seem somewhat ... inadequately dressed," she said a little hesitatingly.

"You mean I have no coat?" Kane replied.

She nodded.

"I just wondered ... if you carried a coat over your arm ... it would look as if you had one ... but felt too hot to wear it."

Kane smiled at her.

"I said you were intelligent, and may I say you are already earning every penny of the salary I have offered you!"

"I would like to think that was true," Octavia replied, "but I still think you are being over-generous."

"We will argue over that later," Kane said. "Please give me the coat you suggest I should carry."

Octavia looked down at her trunk.

She remembered she had packed at the bottom of it her riding-habit.

It was old and almost threadbare because it had in fact belonged to her mother and she had worn it after she had grown out of her own.

But it had been cut by a first-class tailor, and because it was made of good cloth and severe in style it could easily pass as a man's coat rather than a woman's.

She held it out to Kane and knew he was pleased.

When she had pushed in his discarded shirt and fastened her trunk again, she put on the small bonnet in which she travelled and tied the ribbons under her chin.

After she had finished she thought they looked a very ordinary pair of English travellers who might be seen at a railway station or large port in any part of the world.

As Kane walked towards the door she said:

"My brother paid for my accommodation before he left."

"In that case it is quite easy," Kane replied. "I will merely say, if anybody asks questions, which I doubt, that I came here this morning to collect you. Anyway, the Hotels in Alexandria are used to their guests not staying more than one or two nights as they invariably leave quickly either for Cairo or for one of the ships in the harbour."

Octavia picked up her handbag.

As she walked towards the door she thought she was embarking on an incredible and mysterious adventure. It might be very reprehensible of her, but if she refused to partake in it, she knew she would regret it for the rest of her life.

As if once again Kane knew what she was thinking, as he stood holding open the door for her he said:

"You are very brave, and I am thanking Fate, or the gods, that I have been so lucky as to find you!"

chapter three

To Octavia's relief there was no difficulty about leaving the Hotel.

The Concierge confirmed that Tony had paid the bill before he left and he took no notice of Kane, presumably thinking it normal that somebody had come to escort her.

They left the Hotel in an open carriage for hire and which was driven so recklessly through the heavy traffic that Octavia expected every moment they would run over a child or a dog or even one of the men in their *tarbooshes* who seemed determined to be knocked down and injured.

When they reached a narrow street with shops on each side of it Kane told the driver to stop and said to Octavia:

"I shall not be long."

Without explaining any further he got out and went into a shop.

It did not look at all expensive or well stocked, and she wondered what he was seeking.

As soon as they stopped some ragged children ran up to the carriage with outstretched hands begging in whining tones for 'backsheesh.'

Because some of them looked so pitifully thin and in distress Octavia gave them the rest of the few copper *piastres* she had left in her handbag.

Although they seemed delighted at her generosity, she noticed that those she had already rewarded tried to return for more hoping she would not recognise them.

She was growing worried about what Kane was doing when she saw him emerge from the shop carrying a large parcel under his arm.

He climbed back into the carriage and put the parcel on the seat opposite. But as they drove on he made no comment on what he had purchased, and she thought perhaps it would seem impertinent if she asked questions.

They arrived at the station and looking round her curiously Octavia did not overhear what Kane was saying at the Ticket Office.

Here again he seemed to take a long time and she remembered her father had often said that foreigners always took double the time to transact any business and even the best of them were too voluble.

When finally Kane joined her he said:

"We are in luck! There is a train leaving in a quarter-of-an-hour!"

She heard the relief in his voice, and knew once again that he was thinking he was being watched.

He hurried her onto the platform and found her, to her surprise a corner seat in a First Class compartment.

She had somehow expected they would travel Second Class as she had been obliged to do with Tony.

She however, appreciated the comfort of the carriage although there was no corridor and she presumed it was old-fashioned stock.

Kane had seen her trunk into the Guard's-Van, came back to the carriage and shutting the door, stood at the window deliberately looking aggressive so that no other passenger joined them before they left.

Then with clouds of steam and a screeching of wheels the train began to move away from the station.

"There do not seem to be many passengers travelling as grandly as we are!" Octavia said with a smile.

"They have taken the Express which left shortly before we arrived," Kane explained. "However although this is slower I am hoping it will get us there more safely."

She knew by that he was supposing that the men who were following him would have expected him to take the faster train.

She did not make any comment, hoping that now they were alone he would tell her exactly what was happening and why his life was in danger.

As the train gathered speed Kane said:

"I hope you will forgive me if I take the opportunity of sleeping. I did not get any sleep at all last night, and I am, in fact, extremely tired."

"Yes, of course," Octavia agreed.

She thought she too might be more comfortable if she removed her bonnet, so after a moment she took it off.

She got up and stood a little unsteadily in front of a small mirror over the back of her seat.

When she had tidied her hair she looked down to see that Kane, stretched out on the opposite seat, was already asleep.

He had just lain down and fallen asleep immediately, showing that he was indeed, as he had said, very tired.

He had bought two newspapers at the station, one of which was in English, but after reading the headlines Octavia found herself studying the man opposite her and asking herself if she had been wise to trust him to take her to Cairo.

She was quite sure Tony would be very angry if he knew about it, and would tell her she should have obeyed her instructions and gone home.

She also knew her mother would have considered it shockingly reprehensible, and even her father, with his sense of adventure, might have been critical.

But she knew, although she was a little frightened and apprehensive of the trouble she might encounter with Kane Gordon, that she would be far more frightened if, at this moment, she were embarking on a strange ship on which she would then be travelling alone for nearly a week before reaching England.

On the voyage from Tilbury to Alexandria she had taken very little notice of the other passengers.

Now as she thought back, she realised they were mostly men, many of whom were young and, she imagined, Commercial Travellers of some sort.

When they were not being seasick they were flash-
ily dressed and had what was jokingly called a 'roving
eye.'

Octavia had been well aware of the way they had
looked at her and thought it impertinent, but they had
not bothered her because Tony was with her.

She was sensible enough however, to realise that
if Tony had not been there things might have been
very different, and she could have found herself in
some very uncomfortable situations on the voyage
home alone.

She looked at Kane and thought, although she could
not imagine on what grounds, that there was something about him that she trusted.

And after all, if he became difficult or the situation
intolerable, she still had her money intact, and could
leave him.

She would find it more difficult now because she
would have to get back from Cairo to Alexandria, but
she supposed she could manage it, and as she was
likely to be very much alone in the future it was
something she would have to get used to.

Then she wondered what sort of work he wanted
her to do apart from pretending to be his wife, which
was all that at the moment was required.

She hoped that once the men who had been trying
to kill him in Alexandria realised he had escaped, they
would perhaps give up the pursuit and Kane need no
longer be afraid of them.

Then she found herself thinking that if anything
happened to him it would be very, very frightening

57

for her. She might have to explain to the authorities how she was connected with him and why she was pretending to be his wife.

'I must be careful not to let my name appear in the newspapers,' Octavia thought. 'Tony would be furious!'

Then because the scene through which they were passing was so unusual and so exciting she ceased to worry about herself and enjoyed everything she could see from the window.

There was a flat plain burnt by the sun, though in the distance she could see that everything was vividly green and knew that was where the Nile would be.

She had not had any time to learn about Egypt, or to read about it, until she had found herself through the turbulent waters of the Bay of Biscay and halfway to Alexandria.

Then she had found an old guide-book on the ship which she took delightedly into her cabin, and she kept attempting to remember all she had learnt from her Governesses about the Pyramids, the Temples, and of course the opening of the Suez Canal.

Now she did not need the guide-book to describe to her the fertility and beauty of the Nile Delta.

As the train travelled on and she saw the sun illuminating the hills of the desert with a pink light, she could understand how the early Egyptians had regarded it with awe as part of the power of the gods.

She remembered reading that the Pharaohs had likened Egypt to a lotus flower: the fertile but very narrow valley was the stem, the widening Delta was its outspread blossom.

On the other side there was desert land which looked

exactly as Octavia had expected, with its yellow-white sand and rough stones stretching uncompromisingly for miles.

There were also frequent glimpses of rich greenery and she remembered that the life of Egypt lay in the blue waters of the Nile.

She found herself wishing that she could sail up the great river as the ancient Egyptians had travelled when it was not only their country's heartbeat and its strength, but was also its main thorofare.

'Perhaps Kane will take me on the Nile one day,' Octavia thought, then wondered if, when she was working for him, she would have the time.

She wished that Kane would wake up so that she could talk to him.

There were so many things she wanted to know, so many things she wanted him to explain to her, but he lay still with his eyes closed, his face in repose making him look younger than he did when awake.

She thought he must be very strong and also very tough to be able to endure the life he was living without leaving the country, and perhaps going back to England where he belonged.

She found herself insatiably curious to know what was happening, and when they drew into a station she wondered if he would wake up.

The station was not a large one, and the train stopped only for a few minutes.

It appeared that nobody got out, and there were only half-a-dozen passengers waiting to get in.

Then they were off again and because it was very hot Octavia found herself dozing a little. Her thoughts seemed to run into her dreams and it was difficult to know where one ended and the other began.

Then with the usual screech of the brakes and clouds of steam she realised they were coming into a larger station and there were quite a number of passengers on the platform.

They were very colourful, the women in their all-enveloping black or white *burnouses,* their faces covered with a *yachmak* except for their eyes, and the men usually wearing a *gellebryya,* the loose native garment which always looked like a long shirt.

Nobody appeared to be travelling First Class and there was no one on the platform outside their carriage.

Now Kane was awake and rubbing his eyes he said:

"I feel better. Thank you for letting me sleep."

"I could hardly have stopped you," Octavia replied with a smile.

"I am sure most women would have chatted away like parakeets," he replied. "Now as a reward I will give you something to eat, and I am sure you could do with a drink."

He would have opened the carriage door, but Octavia put out her hand.

"Are you wise?" she asked. "Nobody has disturbed us so far . . . but there might be . . . somebody on . . . the train."

He looked at her for a moment. Then he said:

"You are very sensible. Anybody might think you had been in this game for years."

She wondered as he spoke if it really was a game to him, and knew that if it was it was a very dangerous one.

Because he knew she was talking sense, instead of

getting out he called a porter, gave him an order in his own language, and the man hurried away.

He returned with a young man with a white coat carrying a tray on his head.

He handed it through the window to Kane who paid what seemed to Octavia quite a lot of money and tipped the porter who had summoned him.

When the tray was set down in the carriage beside them she found that there was a dish of pigeon which Kane told her was very popular and called 'Hannam.'

It was a little tough but otherwise quite edible, and there was a cheese which she found delicious and some unleavened bread, which Kane said she would have to get used to because she would find it everywhere.

The butter tasted slightly rancid but nevertheless Octavia enjoyed what she thought of as a picnic and the fresh fruit which was delicious.

There was also some fruit juice for them to drink which she had difficulty in recognising because it was a mixture of several fruits.

When they had finished Kane put the tray at the end of the compartment and told her it would be collected at Cairo.

"At what time do we arrive there?" she asked.

"I imagine we should be there soon after four o'clock," he replied.

There was a pause and she wondered if he would tell her what they were going to do when they arrived, and where they would be staying.

But he had a pre-occupied air about him, and she thought perhaps he was still tired and had no wish to answer a lot of questions.

In fact, after sitting up for some minutes he lay down again full length as he had done before, and though he was not sleeping she knew he was thinking and she thought it would be a mistake to interrupt his thoughts.

"I hate women who chatter when I am driving!" her father had often said, and Octavia was sure the same applied to every sort of travelling.

Anyway, the sound of the wheels was very noisy, and she was sure that even though there was nobody to hear them Kane would not wish to shout out his secrets.

She therefore concentrated again on looking out of the window, wondering how soon she would see the Pyramids and what she would feel about them when she did.

She wished in a way they could have stayed longer in Alexandria so that she could visit some of the places her guide-book had told her were worth seeing.

On one thing she was determined: she would not leave Cairo without seeing the Pyramids and the Sphinx.

This was an excitement she had certainly not expected when only a very little while ago she had been sitting by her father's bedside and wondering if he would ever regain consciousness.

"I am living an adventure," she told herself, "and I must enjoy every moment of it. Then when I have to go back to the Priory to live in an empty house and feed myself on potatoes from the overgrown kitchen-garden, then at least I shall have something to remember!"

"Why are you worrying?" Kane asked unexpectedly.

As he spoke Octavia started. She had been so far away in her thoughts that she had almost forgotten he was there.

"How do you know I am worrying?"

"I can feel it vibrating towards me."

"Then, since I do not wish to disturb you, it is something I must stop doing."

"You can stop doing it because I have promised I will look after you," he said. "Trust in me, and although tomorrow may lie in the lap of the gods they are on the whole being very generous."

She knew he was thinking that he was alive when he might easily have been dead by now.

"Perhaps," she said, "I should be . . . taking care of . . . you."

He smiled.

"It is quite a possibility, and you have already shown yourself to be very efficient at that unenviable task."

"Do you think those men will realise you have . . . left Alexandria?" Octavia asked.

It was an unanswerable question and she was not surprised when Kane replied:

"Let us talk about you. That is far more interesting!"

Octavia was just wondering what she should tell him and if it would be a mistake for him to know too much in case he decided she should return to England, when she was aware the train was slowing down.

"We are coming into another station," she said.

Kane sat up.

"Yes, a bigger one," he replied, "and after this it is a straight run through to Cairo."

As Octavia started to peer out of the window Kane lay down again.

"I doubt if there will be many passengers," he said in a sleepy voice.

Octavia did not answer.

She was looking with amusement at the people crowded on the platform, most of whom seemed to have no intention of travelling anywhere, but were staring at the train, or perhaps meeting friends who were on it.

They were colourful, although many of them were ragged and dirty, and they had strange and interesting faces which she thought any artist would want to study and depict.

Then as she leaned further out of the open window, listening to the clamour and watching the women with huge bundles who were clambering into what she was sure were the already over-crowded cheap carriages, she suddenly gave an exclamation and drew back.

"What is it?" Kane asked.

"I think . . . although I cannot be . . . certain that one of the men that came into my . . . bedroom is on . . . the platform!"

Kane sat up but he made no attempt to look out of the window.

"Can you be sure?"

"One of the men had on a coat with a brown and yellow pattern," Octavia said, "and although I was pretending to be half-asleep I thought only somebody very unpleasant would choose anything so ugly."

"And you think he is on this train?"

"He got out of a carriage just behind the engine," Octavia answered, "and I think he was walking in this direction!"

"Shut the window," Kane said sharply, "and go and sit on the other side of the compartment! Look out that way, and whatever happens do not turn your face in this—direction."

Quickly Octavia obeyed him.

As she pushed aside the tray which had held their luncheon so that she could sit in the far corner, she was aware that her heart was beating tempestuously and she was trembling.

If the man saw Kane, what would happen?

She could only pray that he had not seen her as she had seen him.

Although Kane was lying down again full length on the seat, she was aware that he was tense and she felt as if he was waiting for something to happen.

The minutes seemed to crawl past slowly.

Then there was the Guard's whistle, the sound of steam escaping, and with their usual discordant crash the wheels began to turn.

Octavia gave a sigh of relief.

Then as the train began slowly, very slowly to gather speed she turned to look at Kane saying as she did so:

"We are leaving, and perhaps I made...a mistake."

Even as she spoke the door of the carriage was pulled violently open and a man jumped in.

One look at him told Octavia he was one of the men who had come to her bedroom, and it was he who had answered Kane's question as to what they wanted.

For a moment he stood poised against the window as if he was getting his balance.

Then Octavia gave a scream as she saw him draw from the inside of his coat a long, sharp knife which gleamed as he moved it.

Even as he did so, Kane moved too like a tiger from his recumbent position and obviously took the man by surprise.

Then they were fighting desperately, and knowing Kane was unarmed Octavia thought despairingly that he had not a chance.

Then quickly, so quickly that she could hardly believe it had happened, she saw Kane strike with his hand stiff as a ramrod on the back of the man's neck.

As he collapsed onto the floor of the carriage the knife flew out of his hand.

It landed a few inches from her feet, and as she stared down at it wondering if she should pick it up, and yet afraid to do so, Kane opened the door of the carriage and thrust the man's body out through it.

By now the train was well away from the station and travelling at speed along an embankment.

All Octavia knew was that one moment the man's body was in the carriage, next he had gone, and there was only the knife lying at her feet to show what had happened.

Her teeth were chattering as Kane came towards her and she was aware that she was trembling.

"It is all right," he said quietly. "I am sorry you had to see that happen, but at least there is now one fewer of them."

"He is . . . dead?" Octavia asked in a voice that did not sound like her own.

"Yes, he is dead."

Kane picked up the knife, and as he did so Octavia thought it might at this moment be in his body, and he would have been dead instead of the man who had tried to kill him.

She was so frightened that it made her tremble more than ever, and she hoped that Kane would not notice it.

He was however not looking at her, but inspecting the knife, turning it over in his hands as if he thought it might have a name on it or could give him some clue where it had come from.

However he found nothing and opening the window flung the knife out.

For a moment it glinted almost evilly in the sunlight, and then it had vanished in the same way as its owner.

Kane came back and sat down beside Octavia.

"Give me your hand," he said.

She obeyed him and he covered it with both of his.

"I am sorry," he said again.

"I shall be . . . all right . . . in a m—moment."

The words seemed to come jerkily from between her lips, and looking at their luncheon-tray Kane saw there was a little of the fruit juice left.

He picked up the glass and held it to her lips, his other arm supporting her shoulders.

She wanted to refuse, feeling it would be impossible for her to swallow anything.

But he persisted, and because she could not make the effort to thrust him away she drank.

Kane put the glass back down on the tray. Then he said:

"Listen to me, Octavia, I have something important to say to you."

She turned her face towards him and he saw how frightened she was and that her lips were trembling.

His arm tightened around her shoulders.

"What I am going to say," he said quietly, "is that if this is all too much for you and you would rather go back to England, I will arrange it. I will send you to Alexandria with a Courier who will find you a cabin on one of the P. & O. Liners, and he will make sure that you are looked after on your journey home. Is that what you would like to do?"

It took Octavia a second or two to assimilate what he had said.

Then as she thought of being alone, of travelling with a lot of strangers, she replied:

"No . . . no! I am all . . . right! It was just the . . . shock of seeing him . . . fighting with you . . . and think-ing . . . you might be . . . k–killed!"

"You were thinking of me?"

"Of course I was thinking of you. It was . . . my fault he was aware that you . . . were here."

"I think he suspected I might be, and joined the train at the last minute," Kane replied. "If you had not seen him, he would have waited until we arrived in Cairo, and it might not have been so easy to dispose of him there."

He felt Octavia shiver as she remembered how he had thrown the man from the train. Then he said:

"Are you quite sure you prefer to stay with me?"

"Please . . . let me," Octavia begged. "I am afraid

of what will . . . happen when I am with you . . . but I think I am more . . . afraid of travelling such a long way back to England . . . alone."

"I cannot understand why the man you tell me is your brother, left you," Kane remarked.

Because she knew he was criticising Tony, Octavia replied:

"He had to leave me . . . he could not really help it . . . and it is very . . . foolish of me to be . . . afraid. After all, I am nineteen and should be able to . . . look after myself."

"I agree it is an awe-inspiring age!"

She knew he was teasing her and with an effort she said:

"I am all right now. You do not think . . . anybody on the train . . . knows what has happened?"

"I think it is very unlikely," Kane said, "but for your sake, as well as mine, I intend to take every precaution. So we are not going to step out at Cairo looking as we do now."

"What do you . . . mean?"

"I came prepared for something like this."

He took his arm from her shoulder and crossing to the other side of the carriage opened the large bundle he had bought in the shop.

Octavia saw that it contained a black *burnous* such as Muslim women always wore, a *yachmak* to cover the face, and a pair of sandals in which the women in the streets shuffled along.

"I want you to put these on," Kane said, "and I promise you when you do so no one, not even your friend Tony, would recognise you."

Octavia managed to smile.

69

"I am sure . . . that is . . . true."

"Then let me help you," Kane said, "we should be in Cairo in about twenty minutes time."

"Do you think the other man is on the train?" Octavia asked anxiously.

"I have no idea," Kane replied. "That is why we must take no chances. I am only hoping you will not find the sandals too uncomfortable or find it hard to breathe when your face is covered."

Octavia thought she would put up with a great deal of discomfort if it helped her to be less frightened, and that it was best to do what he wanted and not talk about it.

"First," he said, "take all your money and put it in the front of your gown."

Obediently Octavia opened her handbag and took out the £25 which Tony had given her.

She realised as she did so that it was all in English currency, which meant she would have to change some of it, and was sure that at any Hotel she would receive a very bad rate of exchange.

She knew she should have insisted on Tony doing this before he left, but he had been in such a hurry to get back to Virginia Vanderburg that she knew he had not really thought about her seriously.

It was only when Kane had taken off her shoes and put on the shapeless flat-soled sandals that she asked:

"Must we leave our own things behind?"

"It would be best to do so," Kane replied. "In fact, I intend to throw them out of the window."

He thought Octavia was going to protest and added quickly:

"I promise you I will replace everything you lose

70

as soon as we are safely in Cairo."

Octavia hoped he could afford it.

Although her bag was old and the leather had worn at the corners, it was the only one she possessed, and her shoes were her best and most presentable.

But she was still too shaken by what had just happened to argue, and just as she had felt when she first met Kane he seemed to have taken her will from her, and whether she liked it or not, the only thing she could do was to obey him.

She knew she must be unrecognisable in the black enveloping *burnous* which reached nearly to the ground and covered her completely so that there was not a sign of the garment she was wearing beneath it.

Then Kane took from his bundle a small pot of powder. He mixed it with a little of water they had not drunk, and with it tinted her nails and the palms of her hands.

"Now you really look the part," he said. "Nobody will query for a moment that you are not what you appear to be."

"I feel very strange," Octavia confessed.

"As I will keep you company," he said. "I suggest you shut your eyes while I change."

Octavia shut her eyes, and as she did so she prayed their disguises would not be penetrated and nobody would ever learn the extraordinary way she was behaving with a strange man she had met only a few hours before.

"I must just think of it as an adventure," she told herself.

At the same time she shivered as she could see again as if it was still happening, the glinting evil of

71

the Egyptian's eyes as he drew out his knife to kill Kane, and the movement like the leap of a tiger with which Kane threw himself on top of him.

They had indeed fought like two wild animals, until Kane had won and thrown his vanquished enemy out of the train.

"It cannot be . . . true! It cannot . . . really have . . . happened," Octavia murmured.

She felt a sense of panic sweep over her, realising that, while Kane had defeated the would-be assassin, he himself was now a murderer.

'I ought to have . . . told him that I . . . must go . . . home,' she thought, then heard Kane say with a note of laughter in his voice:

"You can look now!"

She opened her eyes and saw why he was amused.

He was wearing the loose cotton *gellebryya* of the Egyptian native, on his head was a *tarboosh*, and on his nose a pair of steel-rimmed spectacles.

He looked so different and so strange that despite all her fears Octavia could only laugh.

"How could you make yourself look like that?" she asked.

"Do you think it is effective?"

"I am sure nobody would ever recognise you."

"That is what we are praying for."

He picked up his clothes which were lying on the seat, together with Octavia's bag and shoes and the coat of her riding-habit which she had lent him.

As she realised what he was going to do she opened her lips to tell him she could not lose her riding-jacket as it was the only one she possessed.

Then she thought he would only tell her again that

he would give her another, and it would be a mistake to argue about it.

He went to the window on the other side of the carriage and threw out the things, one by one.

Octavia felt a little pang of regret as first her hand-bag went, then her riding-coat.

She told herself that it was all part of the incredible sequence of events since her father's death.

What did it matter if she was even more shabby than she had looked these last two years when he never gave her enough money for food, let alone clothes?

Kane came and sat down beside her and taking her hand in his looked at her hennaed nails with what she thought was a twinkle in his eyes.

Then his fingers tightened on hers and he said:

"I suppose you realise that you are a very exceptional person? I know of no other woman, and this is the truth, who could behave as bravely as you have."

"I . . . I was very . . . shocked," Octavia whispered.

"Of course you were!" he answered. "But you did not scream, and you have not raged at me as you might easily have done. One day I will tell you how much you have helped me."

She thought he would say more, but instead he said in a different tone of voice:

"Now, the moment we arrive, while the steam is still pouring out of the engine and making it hard for those at the front of the train to see what is happening, we are going to walk away as quickly as possible and leave the station before anybody is aware of it."

"Supposing the . . . other man is watching?" Octavia asked in a small voice.

"He is . . . unlikely to recognise us," Kane answered, "and he will have no idea what has happened to his confederate in crime."

He spoke so reassuringly that she felt some of the panic within her subside a little.

"And you . . . really think we . . . can get . . . away?" she asked.

"How can we fail? You have been so magnificently brave, and as I told you before, the gods are on my side. They brought me to you, and I cannot believe they will fail me now."

She felt as if his confidence swept away her fears and once again she was thinking of it as an adventure.

"It will certainly be a very exciting . . . story when we reach the . . . last page," she said.

"I can only hope," he replied, "that it is not far ahead."

As he spoke the train began to slow down and Octavia had a glimpse of pointed minarets, of domes and a profusion of white flat roofs outside the window.

They were coming into Cairo. The sky was vividly blue, the sun was shining.

Yet as Kane took her hand and drew her towards the door on the other side of the carriage, she was wondering what unsuspected terror was now waiting for them.

chapter four

As they walked through the seething crowd on the platform, Octavia's heart was beating frantically and her lips felt dry.

She also, as Kane had anticipated, felt suffocated by the *yachmak* over her nose and was afraid that her sandals might fall off.

Now she understood why Eastern women had to shuffle along because the sandals were held on to the feet by strips of leather which were hard and at the same time loose.

As they got out of the train Kane had said:

"Walk a little way behind me which is correct in the East."

She obeyed him, shuffling along as close as she dared, and glad that she was behind him and could keep him in sight.

Then as she wondered in terror if the other man who had come to her bedroom was waiting somewhere along the platform, to kill Kane, she remembered something.

Although her eyes had been half-closed, she had been unable to prevent herself from looking at the Egyptians when Kane was speaking to them in her bedroom.

She had noticed the ugly yellow and brown jacket of the man who was now dead, but when she tried to visualise the other man his face seemed in retrospect to be just a blur with nothing unusual about it.

Then as she tried to force her memory to be more acute, Octavia remembered something very significant about him.

The second man had a scar just below his left eye.

She had not noticed it until the man turned to leave when as he looked back she had noticed without really being aware of it that the scar, showing white against his dark skin, was in the shape of a crescent moon.

She had not thought of it until this moment, but she knew that if she saw the man again with that mark on his face, even if he was disguised she would recognise him.

However she felt too frightened to look for him, and she could only lower her eyes to watch Kane's feet moving along in front of her.

There were a number of people walking in the same direction all round them, until quite suddenly the crowd seemed to thin out, and there was a breath of fresh air as they came outside the station.

With her eyes lowered because she was still afraid of what she might see, Octavia heard Kane hail a carriage and she thought that just as he had altered his appearance, he had also altered his voice.

"He is clever . . . very clever," she told herself and prayed that he would be clever enough to escape another attack on his life.

It was a wonderful relief when she could step into the carriage, and as Kane joined her the horse moved off.

Only when she looked up to be dazzled by the sunshine did she remember her trunk was left behind in the Guard's-Van.

"My clothes!" she exclaimed.

"I will get you new ones," Kane said automatically.

Because it was the inevitable answer she laughed.

Then because he looked surprised she explained through the thickness of her *yachmak*:

"That is what you always say, but there is now a long list of things that will have to be replaced."

"If you are insinuating that I shall not keep my promise," Kane said, "you are mistaken, and I am told there are some very good dressmakers in Cairo."

It flashed through Octavia's mind that they would probably be expensive, but she did not say anything.

She only looked around at the crowded streets through which they were passing, and at the minarets and the domed Mosques silhouetted against the blue of the sky.

She drew in her breath.

"Whatever happens," she exclaimed, "I shall be glad I have seen Cairo!"

"There is a great deal to see which means you will have to stay here for a long time!"

She wondered if he was teasing her or if he really wanted her to stay.

He did not however seem inclined to be conversational, and she therefore concentrated on watching the people on the streets, and wondering how many of them were as dangerous as the man with the crescent mark under his eye.

There was also a great number of British soldiers as Tony had told her there would be.

She tried to remember why they were there and thought she must ask Kane later to explain it to her.

There was so much that she wanted to know, but she was still afraid that now they had reached Cairo he would have no further use for her.

Perhaps in a day or two, he would dispense with her services and she would have to start travelling back to England alone.

She gave an involuntary little shudder at the thought which Kane must have noticed, for he said:

"You are still worried, but we are over the worst of it now, and very shortly we will be able to discard these unattractive garments and be more comfortable."

Octavia did not have to ask the obvious question because he laughed and added:

"I promise I will find you something to wear, and you will be glad to hear that we will not be going anywhere important tonight."

"That is certainly a relief," Octavia replied a little sarcastically.

"I may tell you the reason is not that I am worrying about your appearance," Kane said, "but that I am really tired, and I think we could both do with a good night's sleep."

She knew as he spoke he was laughing at her and she said:

"You at least slept in the train!"

"You shall have your fair share tonight," Kane promised, "and I will ensure that you are not disturbed."

She thought what he said sounded comforting.

They were now crossing a bridge over the Nile, and on the far side there were no shops but only important-looking houses standing back from the road in their own gardens.

Octavia did not ask any questions, but after driving for what seemed a long way down a straight road with trees heavy with blossom, on each side of it, the carriage turned in at a gate.

There was a short drive, and then in front of them was a white Villa surrounded by flowering shrubs and with clematis growing up its walls.

"How pretty!" Octavia exclaimed. "Is this where we are staying?"

"It is a house I share with a friend," Kane replied, "and I make it my home when I am in Cairo!"

It sounded as if he had been here many times before, and Octavia thought this made yet another question she wanted to ask him when she got the chance.

The driver drew up outside a verandah covered with flowering creepers, where stone steps lead up to what was obviously the front door.

Kane got out, helped Octavia to alight, then paid the cabman.

The carriage drove away and they walked up the steps.

Standing inside the door was an Egyptian servant in spotless white bowing low.

"You back, Master!" he exclaimed. "That good!"

"Yes, I am back, Hassam," Kane replied. "Is everything all right?"

"No, Master, bad news!"

Kane was still.

"What has happened?"

"Three men come after you leave. I know they bad so I hide!"

"That was sensible of you."

"They walk in, search every room, find nothing."

"Good!"

Kane moved for the first time since Hassam had been speaking and walked into the house.

The rooms were large, cool and comfortable. Everything gave the impression of being white.

"Cool drinks, Hassam," Kane said, "and quickly!"

"Yes, yes, Master, I very quick!" Hassam promised.

Kane turned to Octavia who was standing looking around her.

"Now you can take off that infernal garment!" he said. "It makes you look like a balloon."

He helped Octavia pull off the *burnous* and she undid the *yachmak* feeling at last she could breathe, although the air was hot and heavy.

She pushed up her hair, finding as she did so that her forehead was damp not only from the heat, but because she had been so frightened.

Then as she sat down on a sofa she kicked off the flat sandals.

"I shall never look at a Muslim woman again," she said, "without feeling that my heart bleeds for her. How can they endure such discomfort every time they leave their home?"

"I suppose they get used to it," Kane replied, "but I prefer you looking as you do now."

"Hot and dishevelled," Octavia smiled.

"I can think of more complimentary adjectives," Kane replied, "but it would be a mistake to make you conceited."

Octavia laughed.

"I am not likely to be that. I have so little to be conceited about."

She did not wait for his answer or note the expression in his eyes.

Instead she got up from the sofa exclaiming:

"I see you have some very interesting treasures, and I suppose some of them came from the tombs."

"Most of them belong to me," Kane said, "and I have been meaning when I have the time to ship them back to England."

"Is that where your home is?"

She was interested, at the same time she thought it would be a mistake to be too curious, in case in return Kane asked her about her home.

To prevent his doing so she said quickly:

"Look at that exquisitely sculptured head! Surely it must be one of the Pharaohs?"

"Actually, it was one of the guardians of a tomb," Kane replied.

He had not moved from the chair in which he was sitting, but was lying back comfortably watching her as she moved around the room.

He had taken off his disfiguring spectacles and the *tarboosh,* and loosened his cotton *gellebryya* at the neck.

"These are very pretty!" Octavia exclaimed.

She was looking at a table on which there was a number of small boxes.

They were laid out, she thought, in the same manner as the collection of snuff-boxes there had been at the Priory before her father had sold them.

These were however much more roughly made. At the same time some were attractive with semi-precious stones inlaid on the lids, and each one had a catch that fastened with a long thin metal pin.

She was touching first one, then the other when Kane rose and walked across the room to stand beside her.

"Do you know what they are?" he asked.

"I cannot think," Octavia replied, "unless they are the boxes in which the wives of the Pharaohs or perhaps their concubines, put the salves and other lotions with which they adorned themselves."

She remembered as she spoke that she had read somewhere that Cleopatra had not only bathed in milk and used honey on her skin, but had many other cosmetics with which she kept herself so beautiful.

"No, you are quite wrong!" Kane replied. "These are in fact small cages in which Ancient Egyptians, and perhaps some of the present ones, kept their scorpions!"

Octavia looked at him in surprise.

"Their scorpions?" she exclaimed. "But I thought scorpions were very dangerous."

"They are indeed!" Kane agreed. "If you are stung by a scorpion you die very quickly and unpleasantly within a few minutes!"

"But why...?" Octavia began.

Then she gave a little cry.

"Are you saying," she asked, "that they kept these on hand so that they could deliberately murder anybody if they felt like it?"

"Exactly!" Kane agreed. "Because some of the boxes are attractive and very valuable I have, as you see, quite a collection of them."

"Now you have spoilt my pleasure at seeing them," Octavia complained, "and I cannot imagine why you should want to collect anything so horrible!"

She walked away from the table as she spoke and Kane followed her.

"I assure you that I would never use one," he said quietly. "I would consider it unsporting."

"You spoke of what you are doing as a game, and that is how you are making it sound," Octavia complained. "But it is wrong and wicked to kill anybody, and I do not want to think about it!"

"I am sorry," Kane said quietly. "I did not mean to upset you, and I realise you have been through a very unpleasant experience already today. Come and sit down to enjoy the drink which Hassam has just brought us. Then I am sure you would like a bath."

He spoke so softly and beguilingly that Octavia felt the anger which had burned within her for a moment ebb away.

But she told herself it was wrong for anybody to speak lightly of murder. Life was so precious, she thought, that it was the ultimate crime to deprive any man of it, however corrupt he might be.

Once again in his uncanny way Kane read her thoughts, and as they sat down at the table on which their drinks were waiting for them he said:

"You are right! Of course you are right, but in this

difficult and often dangerous world in which we live, it is better to laugh than to cry over the foolishness of those who destroy so much that is beautiful."

Octavia looked at him wide-eyed for a moment before she said:

"Then you do . . . understand!"

"I understand, as you do," Kane said, "and while I will try to protect you, you in your turn must try not to be hypersensitive."

"Is that . . . what I am?"

He smiled.

"I know you are. At the same time, you have a self-control which tells me that you are a very exceptional person."

"I wish that were true," Octavia said. "I was thinking when you were asleep in the train how very ignorant I am of so many, many things, and hoping you will find the time to explain them to me."

"That is what I would like to do."

He spoke in a deep voice which gave Octavia a warm feeling inside her.

She gave him a sweet smile as she lifted the long glass of what looked like fruit juice to her lips.

As soon as she sipped it she knew it had been made with limes, and was cool, delicious and thirst-quenching.

She had not realised how thirsty she was until she had drunk nearly half the glass and saw with delight there was a large jug of the juice on the table, so they could both drink as much as they wished.

She realised that since they had entered the Villa it had become much less hot than it had been.

The sun was sinking low in the sky and the shadows

outside in the garden were lengthening.

Kane drank a little more from his glass. Then he said:

"Come upstairs where I am sure Hassam has prepared a bath for you, and I will find you a *caftan* to wear at dinner. Directly after that you must go to bed."

"That all sounds perfect," Octavia smiled.

She drained her glass of lime juice, then followed Kane who was already walking ahead of her up the short staircase to the floor above.

He opened the door of a room that was also painted white with a four-poster bed hung with muslin curtains and on the top of it a mosquito net was gathered.

To Octavia's disappointment there was no bath ready for her in the room.

She had expected that in a private house a lady would bathe in her own bedroom, as in England, since it was considered immodest for her to walk about the corridors in her night-attire.

She knew it was different in Hotels where there were bathrooms which served a number of bedrooms, but she had thought in Kane's villa she would have a bath in her bedroom.

She must have looked surprised for Kane said:

"As I helped design this Villa I had the idea that it would be much more pleasant for me and my main guests to have their own bathrooms."

"It certainly sounds very luxurious!" Octavia replied.

She followed him across the room as he opened a door which revealed a small bathroom.

The bath itself was sunk low into the floor like those she had seen in pictures of Roman baths, and the walls were decorated with an Egyptian mural which was very attractive.

"How lovely!" she exclaimed. "And how very, very clever of you to think of this!"

"I am glad you appreciate it," Kane said. "Enjoy your bath and I will see that when you come out there will be something to wear lying on your bed."

He walked away as he spoke and left her.

Octavia felt as if she had suddenly stepped into a story of the *'Arabian Nights'* and the adventures in which she was taking part grew every moment more surprising.

She took off her gown and hung it in a cupboard which she found had been skilfully built into a wall so that it was not obtrusive like an ordinary wardrobe.

Then she went into the unusual bathroom and lay in the cool water which she found was scented with jasmine.

Everything about Kane was so unexpected, she thought, that the number of questions she wanted to ask him increased every time that her curiosity was aroused.

Because she was so eager to see him again, she did not stay in the bath for long but stepped out of the water and started to dry herself.

Only when she went from the bathroom into the bedroom did she see what he had meant when he said there would be something waiting for her to wear on the bed.

She recognised an Egyptian *caftan* and thought it was something she would love to own.

Of heavy silk in Nile blue it was embroidered with silver thread and tiny pearls.

When she looked at herself in the mirror she thought she might have stepped out of a painted frieze, a reincarnation of an Egyptian woman who had lived thousands of years ago.

Only her hair and her eyes were the wrong colour.

Then she wondered why Kane should have a *caftan* in the house, and if he had bought it for somebody waiting for him in England, perhaps somebody he loved.

The idea, although she did not understand why, seemed somehow disturbing, and she quickly rearranged her hair.

As well as the *caftan* there was a pair of embroidered slippers and as they were made in the form of mules they fitted her regardless of whomever they had been intended for.

As she opened the door and went down the stairs she suddenly felt a little shy.

For the first time it had occurred to her that Kane was a man whom women found attractive, and perhaps they had stayed with him in this Villa and he would not find her as amusing as they had been.

She walked down the stairs slowly, and only when she reached the hall was she aware that he was standing just inside the open doorway watching her.

He had come in from the garden and she saw he was wearing, instead of the conventional evening-dress she might have expected, a white suit and, as if to make it look more appropriate for dinner, a bow-tie.

As she walked towards him she found herself, for no reason she could put a name to, blushing.

As if he understood what she was feeling he said:

"You look very lovely, as I expected you would, and Egyptian dress is surely very suitable seeming that we are in Cairo."

"It is very exciting to be here," Octavia said. "At the same time, everything is so unexpected that it makes me feel breathless!"

"I am hungry," Kane said, "and I am sure you are, as we only had a light luncheon."

He led the way as he spoke into the Dining-Room with long windows opening out onto the verandah and a table in the centre of it with a *punkah* above it moving to fan the air.

Kane sat down at the head of the table and Octavia sat on his right.

Hassam brought them first cold soup which she found was made of cucumbers and was very delicious.

He poured some golden wine into their glasses, and when he had left them Octavia asked:

"Does Hassam do everything in the house?"

"He is in charge of it," Kane answered, "and as he has been with me for a long time he knows exactly what I want. But as in most Egyptian households his family live in a house at the end of the garden, and they all help when it is necessary. I suspect Hassam's brother has cooked our dinner for us, and his son is working the *punkah*."

Octavia laughed.

"No wonder you are comfortable!"

"Of course!" Kane replied. "There is no point in being uncomfortable unless one has to be!"

She looked at him for a moment. Then she asked:

"When are you going to explain to me what happened last night and why with a house like this you were escaping over the roofs of Alexandria, and sliding down a dirty drain-pipe?"

It seemed incredible as she spoke the words, just as what had happened afterwards seemed so amazing that it was difficult to believe she had not dreamt it all.

"I will tell you what you want to know after dinner," Kane promised.

The dinner however took a long time.

There was fresh fish from the Nile, quails from the desert, and exotic fruit which Octavia had never heard of let alone tasted before.

After that there was a cup of sweet Turkish coffee which Hassam brought onto the verandah.

By now darkness had fallen, the sky was brilliant with stars, and it was much cooler than it had been all day.

It was very quiet in the garden except for the sound of the crickets and an occasional rustle amongst the shrubs, as if caused by some small animal.

"I always imagined Egypt would be like this," Octavia said dreamily. "I feel as if the air itself is centuries older than any other air, and if I am not careful I shall step back in time and lose the modern world for ever!"

"You will certainly feel like that when I take you to see the Pyramids," Kane said quietly.

"You will not forget?"

"Of course not!"

With what was an effort Octavia forced herself to think of the present, and sitting back comfortably in a big white wicker armchair which was lined with cushions she said:

"Please tell me now what I want to know. Otherwise when I go to bed I shall lie awake wondering about you instead of sleeping."

"Now I think you are trying to blackmail me," Kane said, "but it is only fair that you should know a little of what is happening, although it is not easy to explain it in just a few words."

"Please try," Octavia pleaded.

"I do not know what you know about the political situation in Egypt at the present time?" Kane began.

"I can answer that quite easily," Octavia answered, "nothing!"

"Then I must explain that fifteen years ago Arabi Pasha, an Egyptian, started a rebellion against the Egyptian Government. The British intervened and attacked from the Suez Canal, defeating him at the battle of Tel-el-Kabir and established the British presence in Egypt."

"Did the Egyptians in general accept this?" Octavia asked.

"They were delighted at the time because they knew that otherwise there would have been complete chaos. The Khedive asked that British troops should stay to support him in restoring law and order."

"So that is why there are so many British here!"

"Exactly! Six thousand of them!"

"As many as that?"

"They are all under the control of Lord Cromer whom you shall meet. He is a man of great authority and, although the Khedive sits on the throne, so to speak, Lord Cromer effectively is the Ruler of Egypt."

"I suppose that is what one might have expected," Octavia remarked. "Papa said the British were intent on ruling the whole world before they had finished!"

Kane laughed.

"They have only managed to rule over a quarter of it so far, but there is no knowing where their ambitions will end."

"And where do you come into this?"

"That is quite easy to explain," Kane replied. "I am actually an Archaeologist."

"An Archaeologist?"

Whatever Octavia had expected, it was not this.

"It is a pursuit to which I have applied myself for the last five years," Kane explained, "and it has not only given me an enjoyment which is hard to express, but I have also been, if I may say so, extremely successful."

"What have you found? What have you discovered?"

"A number of things which I will tell you about later. But what concerns us at the moment is that I had to go home temporarily and while I was away my chief assistant whom I left in charge, a very reliable and experienced man, came upon a tomb which he is quite certain will, when it is excavated, reveal treasures of antiquity and value that will astound the whole world."

"It sounds absolutely thrilling!" Octavia exclaimed.

While Kane was speaking she had sat up in her chair and turned to face him.

Her face was raised to his, her hands clasped together in her excitement.

"I had to go home to Scotland because my father had died," Kane said, "and when I returned a fortnight

91

ago I found a letter from my colleague, whose name is Manton, telling me what he had discovered, but warning me there was trouble."

"What sort of trouble?" Octavia asked.

"He was not certain what this would be, but he was obviously very perturbed, and he sent me a map to show where he had found the tomb. But for reasons he did not explain in detail he had, after a quick investigation, stopped digging and covered his tracks by moving on to another site."

"I suppose he was waiting for your return," Octavia suggested.

"That was what I guessed. At the same time, Manton warned me there were men determined to snatch the treasure from us if they could, and use it for their own political aims."

"Political?" Octavia asked.

"That is what Manton said, and since my return I have found that exactly describes the situation."

"But since you came back has he not explained more fully what he meant?"

"That was of course what I had expected him to do," Kane said, "but he has disappeared!"

"Disappeared?"

"After he wrote the letter to me enclosing the map of the exact location of the tomb, he had not been seen again."

Octavia stared at Kane wide-eyed.

"Are you . . . suggesting," she asked in a low voice, "that he has been . . . killed?"

"No," Kane replied, "but I think he has been kidnapped."

"But . . . why?"

"I have of course made full investigations among those who know the secrets which are hidden from ordinary people," Kane said, "but are part of Egyptian life and Egyptian thinking."

"Explain to me," Octavia begged.

"Well, the picture at the moment is that a certain person, and we are not sure exactly who he is," Kane said, "except that he is a follower of Arabi Pasha, who is exiled in Ceylon, is determined to throw out the British and the present Egyptian Government headed by the Khedive and continue the anti-foreigner revolution that was put down fifteen years ago."

"Can he do that?"

"He can try," Kane replied, "but first he needs money and a great deal of it."

Octavia thought for a moment before she said:

"I presume he thinks he can get that from the tomb."

"That is intelligent of you," Kane replied. "There are at the moment, more and more people all over the world interested in Egyptian antiques, especially the Americans whose purses are very long."

Octavia thought of Virginia and knew that she was typical of the new type of Americans who were interested in the world outside their own country.

They wanted to take back to the New World the spoils of ancient civilisations to impress their friends.

"Having enough money if he finds the tomb," Octavia asked, "what then?"

"Then I think he will attempt to assassinate Lord Cromer and the present Khedive and place himself in the seat of power."

Octavia gave a deep sigh.

"It sounds terrifying! But why should he want to kill you?"

"That is a question I have of course asked myself," Kane replied. "I have in fact a reputation for being able to discover the details of such plots where other investigations have failed."

"Is the situation very dangerous?"

"Very, as you have already seen!"

Octavia thought for a moment. Then she said:

"But if the revolutionaries kill you, it would not follow that they will get the map of the tomb."

"That is another question I have asked myself," Kane replied. "I think the answer is that they hold Manton as a prisoner and are perhaps torturing him to make him show them where the tomb is situated."

"Torturing . . . him?" Octavia whispered.

"It is something at which the Egyptians are quite skilful," Kane answered, "but they are also aware that a man of Manton's character is completely loyal to those for whom he works and who pay him."

"Which is you!"

"Yes, and I believe, although I may be wrong, that the man who is planning all this thinks that if I were dead, there would be no reason why quite honourably Manton should not work for anyone else prepared to pay him handsomely. It is therefore imperative that I should die!"

Octavia gave a cry of horror.

"But you cannot let him kill you. And if he gets possession of the tomb and the fortune it holds he will then be able to drive out the British!"

"That is what he wants," Kane said, "and so you

do see it is rather important for me to remain alive?"

"Of course it is!" she said.

Kane looked out in the direction of the shrubs under which the shadows were dark and at the trees silhouetted against the sky.

Then he said quietly:

"What I have told you depends to a certain extent on guess-work. However, as I am working it out, step by step, I think my assumptions are correct, and the big prize at the end of the whole operation is to be able to pay enough Egyptians to fight against the British Forces."

"Then they will put Arabi Pasha or his friend back on the throne?"

"They need guns, rifles and a great deal of modern equipment if they are to make any sort of impact on the British Regiments stationed here," Kane said as if he was speaking to himself. "But most of all they need to get rid of Cromer."

"He is so important?" Octavia asked.

"He is the crux of the whole situation. It is difficult for anybody to understand how brilliant he has been in ensuring that Egypt under him has escaped bankruptcy and actually produced an increase in production."

Kane looked towards Octavia to see if she was listening before he went on:

"He has undertaken great irrigation projects such as the Aswan Dam, the railways are being rebuilt, the Egyptian Law-Courts reformed. It would be a disaster of the greatest magnitude if anything should happen to him."

"I can understand that," Octavia said softly, "and

I also think it would be a . . . disaster if anything happened to . . . you!"

Kane smiled. Then in a different tone of voice he asked:

"Do you mean that?"

"Of course I mean it!" Octavia said. "I think that you have under-estimated to me your importance in this fantastic story."

"I think my real importance is that I should stay alive."

As Kane spoke he stretched his arms above his head, at the same time looking up at the stars.

"We all ask ourselves sometimes what is our fate," he said quietly, "and I am very anxious to know mine."

Then he laughed.

"At the moment, more important than anything else is that you and I should both get a good sleep. God knows what tomorrow will bring, but today has definitely been very tiring."

What had taken place certainly seemed incredible, Octavia thought.

First his escape from the roofs, then the way he had turned to her for help, the fight with the man in the train whom he had killed, and the clever manner in which he had got them out of the station disguised and avoiding any more trouble.

"Yes, we must go to bed," she said. "I can see you are going to need all your wits about you."

"Now that you know the truth," Kane said, "are you still going to stay and help me?"

"I want to, but I feel very inadequate, and I am so . . . afraid that I may fail you."

He shook his head.

"I am using my perception, as I did this morning when I glimpsed your golden head through the open door of your bedroom, when I tell you that you are very, very necessary to me."

"Then you must . . . tell me what I am to do . . . and I will . . . do it," Octavia said.

"Thank you."

Kane put out his hand and as she rested hers on it, his fingers closed over hers.

"I want you to stay with me," he said.

A deep note in his voice that had not been there before made her feel her shyness seep over her again.

Then still holding onto his hand she rose to her feet.

"I am going to pray very, very hard that you will be safe, successful, and save Lord Cromer," she said.

"That is what I want you to do," Kane said. "At the same time, as I wish you to have all your wits about you, hurry upstairs and go to bed. It will all seem less frightening and far easier to cope with in the morning."

"I hope so," Octavia replied, "and thank you for . . . letting me . . . stay."

She looked up at him with a smile.

Although he did not move she had the strange feeling that he was drawing her to him, pulling her although why she did not understand.

Then he raised the hand he held in his, kissed it lightly, and said:

"Goodnight, Octavia. I promise you nothing and *nobody* will disturb you tonight."

He seemed to emphasize the word 'nobody,' and she wondered of whom he was thinking.

Then because she was so tired that her head seemed to be full of cotton-wool, she turned and walked from the verandah through the open door through the hall and up the stairs.

When she reached her own room she found that there was a thin lawn nightshirt—she presumed one that belonged to Kane—lying on the turned-down bed.

Because she was too tired to think about the strange tale Kane had just unfolded to her, or even about him, she took off her clothes, put on the nightshirt, crept under the mosquito net which had now been let down, and slipped into the bed.

It was very soft and comfortable, and almost before she had time to pull the sheet, for it was too hot to need anything else, over her she was asleep.

* * *

Kane, despite the fact he had said he was so tired, sat for a long time on the verandah after Octavia had left, looking out into the darkness.

chapter five

OCTAVIA awoke with a feeling of happiness that something exciting was going to happen.

When she opened her eyes and saw the sun coming into her room through the curtains she knew her happiness was because she was in Egypt.

She had slept peacefully and had awoken now only because after a soft tap on the door Hassam had come into the room bringing her breakfast.

He set it down beside the bed, rolled back the mosquito net onto the canopy overhead, and drew the curtains.

Then he raised the sun-blind so that the whole room was flooded with a golden light.

"Nice morning, Lady!" Hassam said. "Master eat good breakfast—go out."

"He has gone out!" Octavia exclaimed.

Now she was suddenly afraid that the man with the scar under his eye was waiting to kill him.

"Master safe," Hassam said as if he knew what she was thinking. "He come back luncheon."

With that he left the room and Octavia lay back against the pillows thinking how comfortable she was.

The room was so beautiful, and she knew it was a joy in itself not to have to cook her own breakfast and saw that what was waiting for her on the tray looked very appetising.

Because Kane would be out until luncheon-time she knew there was no hurry for her to get up and she would be wise to rest while she had the opportunity.

She found herself wondering what sort of work he could be requiring her to do, and felt again how hopelessly unqualified she was to help him, except when he was forced to be disguised, and that could hardly happen every day.

She was still trying to puzzle out for herself what she could do and if she would ever be worthy not of the salary that Kane had offered to pay her, but even of half of it, when Hassam came back into the room.

He took her tray and put it outside. Then he said:

"Lady like bath? Then dressmakers come."

"Dressmakers?" Octavia exclaimed, a little lilt in her voice, and knew that Kane had not forgotten his promise.

Half-an-hour later the dressmaker, who was a very elegant French-woman with two Egyptian girls in attendance, brought her a number of gowns to choose from.

There was also such a large selection of exquisite underclothes and nightgowns that Octavia said quickly that she could not afford to have them.

"*Monsieur* Gordon arrange, *Madame,*" the French-woman said, "all *Madame* 'as to do ees to choose which gowns she like best, and which we make for 'er."

Because she was a very good saleswoman and also very definite as to what her instructions were, Octavia found herself meekly agreeing to accept four day-gowns, and four very elaborate and beautiful evening-gowns.

There were also all the accessories to go with them: shoes, stockings, gloves, handbags, and pretty sun-shades that she could hold over the straw hats trimmed with flowers or feathers.

Only when box after box had been brought in from the carriage in which they had come and the whole room looked like a sale-room, did Octavia say firmly:

"These are the things I would like, but first I must speak to Mr. Gordon before I make a final decision."

She thought the dressmaker looked surprised and added quickly:

"I am sure he is back by now, and if you wait here I will go and find out."

She ran down the stairs, and as she reached the hall saw to her relief outside the open front door Kane stepping out of a carriage.

As he came up the steps and across the verandah she went towards him.

"Good-morning, Octavia!" he said. "I see you have on a new gown, and I am sure you expect me to tell you it is very becoming."

Because she had been worrying about the bill Octavia had forgotten that she had on a thin muslin gown embroidered with a pattern of flowers and with her small waist encircled by a very expensive-looking satin sash.

She clasped her hands together.

"The dressmaker is here," she said, "and she is trying to persuade me to buy far more than I can allow you to pay for."

Kane smiled.

"I gave her my orders, Octavia," he said, "and I can only hope the woman is carrying them out efficiently."

Octavia reached out to put her hand on his arm.

"Please listen to me," she said. "It is very kind of you to offer to replace the things that were lost, and those I must accept. But I have never owned anything so beautiful or so expensive as all the things which are upstairs."

She paused before she added:

"It would be much more economical if you bought one good gown for me, then arranged to have it copied."

She remembered that her mother had said once that tailors in the East could copy any gown so cleverly and so efficiently that if there was a darn on it, or a small hole they even included that.

Kane smiled down into her worried eyes.

"Standing for fittings is always a bore," he said, "and you forget this is one of the ways I can thank you for saving my life."

As Octavia still looked indecisive he said:

"Just tell the dressmaker to carry out my orders. Meanwhile I am hungry and do not want to wait for luncheon."

The way he spoke made it impossible for Octavia to argue with him any further.

She ran back upstairs feeling there were wings on her heels to tell the dressmaker that she would keep all the things she had chosen.

Delighted, and expressing her thanks most volubly, the dressmaker and her assistants left with the promise that the two or three things which had to be altered would be sent back later in the day.

Octavia ran downstairs again anxious to be with Kane.

He was, as she expected, sitting on the verandah with a long cool drink in his hand, and she realised when she looked at him that he too appeared very different this morning.

He was now wearing an exceedingly smart white tussore suit, a tie which she thought was a Regimental one, a silk shirt with gold cuff-links, and highly polished shoes. He certainly looked very different from the man who had come into her bedroom to beg her to help him.

Hassam brought her a drink, and as Octavia was trying to express her thanks for her new wardrobe of clothes he announced that luncheon was ready.

"Tell me what you have been doing," she said when they sat down, thinking it was a mistake to go on talking about herself.

"I have been catching up with what has happened since I left Cairo," Kane replied.

When Hassam left the room she asked in a low voice:

"Is there any news of your friend Mr. Manton?"

Kane shook his head.

"Nothing positive, but those who are in on the secret are as convinced as I am that he is being held prisoner until I am dead."

Octavia gave a little cry of horror.

"If that is true, then surely you should go away, or else be in a much safer place than this?"

"I am quite safe here and so are you," Kane replied. "Although you may not be aware of them, there are people guarding us very efficiently and I promise you no one can get into the house unnoticed."

He spoke in his usual quiet, calm voice and Octavia felt it was impossible to be as afraid as she thought she ought to be.

At the same time, she could not help feeling that with all the windows open onto the garden it would be very easy for somebody to shoot him if they were hiding in the shrubs.

"I promise you are safe," Kane said as if he was following her thoughts.

"I do not... matter. I was thinking of... you."

"Am I really that important?"

"You know you are," Octavia said simply. "I feel so deeply involved with what you are trying to do that I am trying desperately to help, although I feel there is no way I can contribute except by... praying."

"I am very grateful for your prayers," Kane said, "and as you have saved me twice, I cannot believe you would fail me a third time."

Octavia wished to argue that the second time was really her fault for having attracted the killer by looking out of the window.

Then she remembered it might have been impossible for Kane to dispose of him if he had waited until they were leaving the platform.

Because even to think of it made her frightened she said quickly:

"What are you going to do this afternoon?"

"Do?" Kane enquired.

"Oh, please, I want to go with you."

She spoke impulsively, then thought perhaps she was being pushing, and Kane would rather be doing things without her.

But he was smiling and after a moment he said:

"As it is very hot I suggest that after luncheon we sit quietly on the verandah and either read or talk. Then later, in the cool of the evening, I will take you to see the Pyramids."

"Will you really do that?" Octavia exclaimed. "It is what I have been longing for."

"Then that is what we shall do," Kane promised and thought the excitement in her eyes was very touching.

As they sat quietly on the verandah, with the *punkah* moving slowly over their heads, Octavia could hardly believe she had nothing to do but lie back against the soft cushioned seat with her feet raised in front of her.

At the Priory, apart from the fact that she had to keep going into her father's room to see if he was conscious and needed her, there had always been something to clean.

There had been the kitchen, the Sitting-Room she was using, and the passages which seemed to grow longer and dustier every day because she herself was so tired.

Then there had been the clothes to wash because

105

Mrs. Coles was incapable of doing them, and she could not afford to pay a woman who would be more expensive.

Apart from all this there had been the endless battle to find enough to eat.

Their last gardener had retired to the cottage in which he now lived because they could not afford to employ him any longer.

When his rheumatism allowed him to do so, he planted a few vegetables in the garden and occasionally dug up the potatoes for Octavia.

But she usually had to do that herself, just as she had to search among the weeds to find any other vegetables which had come up spontaneously rather than because they had been planted in the spring.

But she had been lucky that the apple, plum and damson trees, old and unpruned, still produced fruit.

She had made a pact with the village boys who had nothing to do, that if they were allowed to snare rabbits in the woods in which in the past they had never been allowed to trespass, they would give her one out of every five rabbits they caught.

Because they kept their word punctiliously there was always a rabbit to eat at the Priory, and sometimes a farmer would bring her a pigeon or a duck.

Although she was grateful she found it very tiring having to pluck them and really preferred the rabbits for which she paid the boys a penny each to skin them.

When she was alone she found it easier to live mostly on eggs which came from the few old hens which wandered about the garden, or which when her father sent her any money she bought locally from the farm.

When Tony came home he always complained about the food, and she could not help feeling when her father was unconscious that it was fortunate he did not have to eat their very meagre meals, which were the best she could provide.

"What are you thinking about?" Kane asked suddenly. "I can see it is worrying you."

"I was thinking of my home," Octavia replied involuntarily.

"Tell me about it."

For a moment she thought she would confide in him. Then she shook her head and said:

"I do not want to think unhappy things."

"I am curious as to why your home should have been unhappy, and why you should leave it to come to Cairo with somebody who abandoned you as soon as you arrived."

There was an undoubted note of condemnation in Kane's voice, and she knew he was shocked that Tony should have left her so quickly.

She still had not the slightest idea that he suspected that Tony was not her brother, but had been in a very different position in her life.

She had noticed that he had referred to Tony as her 'friend' but she had not thought about it again.

"Please, please, let us talk about Egypt," she begged. "I am so frightened that you may suddenly find I am no longer any use to you and will send me home! Then I shall always regret my ignorance about it, and that I have been unable to ask you."

Kane laughed. Then he said:

"I think at the moment, because you are very sensitive, there is no need for words. You can feel you are in what the Greeks called the 'City of the Sun' which for over a thousand years has entranced and intrigued those who visit it."

"It certainly ... entrances and ... intrigues me!"

Somehow she persuaded Kane to talk a little of his archaeological discoveries in the desert, with the promise that tomorrow or the next day he would show her many of the treasures which were at the moment stored in a safe place.

The Egyptians had discovered that anything that could be described as 'antique' had a value not only for the ordinary tourists, but also for the collectors from America and many countries in Europe.

This resulted in them digging indiscriminately, chiselling off friezes and paintings on the walls of any tomb they could break into, and also of course, stealing from any archaeologist who left his discoveries unguarded.

"And nobody stops them?" Octavia asked.

"I assure you we do our best, but the Egyptians are light-fingered as a race and many of them are so poor that one can hardly blame them for stealing when they get the chance."

Octavia smiled. Then she said:

"I know how much it must hurt you to lose things which are part of history, especially to people who do not really appreciate them."

"That is true," Kane agreed, "and what is so fantastic is that after the passage of thousands of years

Egypt is still a treasure-chest of the most fantastic and wonderful sculptures, paintings and jewellery that so far has evaded the thieves."

"It sounds very romantic!"

"That is what I find," he said simply.

As he spoke Octavia wondered if he would ever allow her to go with him to the tomb he was excavating.

If he did, she thought, it would be the most thrilling experience that could happen to her.

Then she thought despairingly that he was unlikely to want a woman with him, and even if she were still in Egypt when he started digging again, she expected she would be left behind.

They sat talking as the afternoon passed and she listened absorbed, not only because what he was telling her was so interesting, but because it was so wonderful to be able to talk to anybody so intelligent.

He also apparently valued her opinions.

Her father had expected her to listen to him, but she had always had the feeling he would rather have been talking to one of the beautiful ladies whom he entertained in London.

Or he preferred a man of his own age who would laugh at his jokes and admire him as a sportsman.

Tony was the same, except that he sometimes confided to Octavia what he had been doing and boasted of his social success.

Sometimes she wondered despairingly if he really thought she had any brains, or if he just made the best of her because there was no one else.

But Kane talked to her as if recognising that she

was intelligent, and she instinctively knew that he enjoyed explaining things to her that she did not understand.

She could hardly believe it was possible when as the sun began to sink lower in the sky he said:

"As I want you to see the sun set behind the Pyramids, I am going to order a carriage, and we will leave in ten minutes."

"That will be thrilling!"

She jumped to her feet and asked:

"What shall I wear? Shall I put on a hat?"

Kane smiled.

"If you want to look smart and impressive you shall certainly wear one. But I like your hair just as it is. Come as you are."

Octavia ran upstairs and collected a light shawl in case it was cold when the sun went down.

Then as she looked in the mirror it was hard to believe it was really herself.

Never had she owned such a beautiful, expensive and elaborate gown.

Because there was a French *chic* about it, it accentuated the slim lines of her figure, the tininess of her waist, and gave her a grace which she had not been conscious of before.

She liked too to hear the rustle of her silk petticoat as she ran up and down the stairs and to know, although it seemed very extravagant, there was real lace on her chemise.

Besides those that were made of fine lawn, the dressmaker had also provided some in silk.

"They will cost Kane a tremendous amount of money!" she said and thought it was very reprehensible that he should pay for such things.

At the same time, what could she do but accept his kind offer?

She wondered what had eventually happened to her trunk, when it had remained in the Guard's-Van unclaimed.

She thought a little wryly that anybody who stole it would not be very excited by its contents.

Then because Kane was waiting she hurried down the stairs and stepped into the open Victoria that was outside the front door.

It was very different from the ramshackle vehicle in which they had driven from the station.

This one was obviously privately owned, and she thought perhaps it belonged to Kane.

It was drawn by two perfectly matched horses and the coachman on the box was well dressed.

She thought it was a mistake to ask too many questions, so she made no comment.

Instead she looked around her with delight as they drove out onto the road which she knew led in the direction of the desert and the Pyramids.

There were trees lining the roadside and a profusion of flowering shrubs.

The colours seemed to blend with the blue of the sky and the gold of the sun to make everything appear even more vividly beautiful than Octavia could ever have imagined.

When finally the houses were left behind and in front of them stretched the silver sands of the desert she had her first glimpse of the Pyramids.

They stood on the rising ground overlooking the Nile Valley and as she looked at them in wonder because it was impossible to speak she slipped her hand into Kane's.

Then he began to talk quietly of what she was seeing, and it was almost as if his words were music to which she responded not with her mind, but with her heart and soul.

"The Pyramids," he was saying, "are a testament to the Ancient Egyptians' belief in the immortality of the soul."

He was silent for a moment. Then he asked:

"Tell me what you feel as you look at them."

"I think at first I felt surprise, because although I had read about them and seen illustrations of them, they are . . . now that I am looking at them . . . different."

"In what way?"

"I feel I am seeing them not . . . with my eyes . . . but with something . . . inside me that recognises them not just as a monument built by men's brains but as if they were built by their . . . spirits . . . or I should say . . . their souls."

She made a little gesture as she said:

"It is hopeless to explain, but to me they are very . . . emotional . . . and yet it is something deeper . . . even than feeling . . ."

Her voice died away and she said helplessly:

"There are no . . . words to describe it . . . and what I am saying does not make sense."

"It makes sense to me," Kane said, "because it is what I feel myself. The first time I saw the Pyramids I knew that while I had a private satisfaction in their elementary simplicity, and perhaps a feeling of awe at the fact that humans could achieve anything so magnificent, yet there was still something else."

"The spirit of life!" Octavia said quietly.

"Exactly!" Kane agreed. "And that is what I knew you would feel."

She did not ask him how, but as they drew a little nearer Kane ordered the carriage to a standstill and they sat in it with Octavia still holding onto his hand.

The sun sank lower, and now the sky was a blaze of brilliant colour.

The crimson of it was now changing to a translucent gold until on the edge of it Octavia could see faintly the first evening star.

It was so beautiful that she felt as if her whole being was lifted up and she was almost disembodied, floating on the music which came from herself to join with a chorus of voices that came from some unknown choir hidden behind the great pointed edifices in front of them.

Only as the sun sank lower still and there was just one crimson line on the horizon did Octavia draw in her breath.

She felt as if she had been transported a million miles to a strange, unknown country in which she had experienced for a moment the perfection of beauty.

Then as she came back to earth she realised she was holding Kane's hand so tightly that she was hurting her own fingers.

She turned to look at him with an apology on her lips.

She found his eyes were on her face: he had been watching her and, she thought, understanding as nobody else would have done what she was feeling.

He did not speak except to order the coachman to drive on, and now, as the last glimmer of the sun vanished, the darkness of the night came swiftly, as it always does in the East.

It was with a pang of regret that Octavia thought that the curtain had fallen and they would go home.

But instead the carriage travelled on and as they drove in silence she knew without being told that Kane was taking her to see the Sphinx.

It grew darker, until it seemed as if the horses found their way by instinct rather than by sight.

Every moment more and more stars were coming out in the sky and the great arc of them overhead seemed to Octavia to fill the whole world so that there was only the stars, herself, and Kane—nothing else.

They drove on until suddenly she saw looming ahead of her something large.

It was difficult to see until the carriage stopped and as it did so, as if it was at Kane's command, the moon came from behind a cloud.

It was a full moon, and as the light grew stronger and stronger Octavia could see very clearly the body of the lion, symbol of Kingship, with a woman's head.

Then for the first time since they had started to move again Kane spoke.

"She faces East," he said quietly, "to watch the rising sun which heralds the return of life."

"Which . . . means that we . . . never die!"

"Of course!"

He opened the carriage door as he spoke and helped Octavia down onto the sandy ground.

Then the carriage drove on a little way, and they walked until they stood alone looking up at the Sphinx's head silhouetted against the sky above them.

Octavia drew in her breath.

It was all that she had expected, all that she had wanted to see, and so much more.

She felt as if the Sphinx had a message for her and she only had to listen while her vibrations reached out to meet the vibrations of the strange, beautiful enigma which had stood there for so many thousands of years.

Then as she tipped up her head and the moonlight played on her face, she felt Kane draw nearer to her.

"It is . . . lovely!" she murmured, "so unbelievably lovely that I . . . feel it cannot be real . . . and yet in my heart I know it is!"

"That is what I feel too," he said in a deep voice.

He put his arms around her as he spoke.

Then as Octavia turned to look at him in surprise his lips came down on hers.

It was not what she expected, not what she had even thought might happen.

Yet as he held her close to him and her lips were soft beneath his, it was part of the beauty of the sunset, the mysteriousness of the Pyramids and the feeling of light that came from the Sphinx.

It was all of these things, but as his lips which had at first been very gentle became more demanding, more possessive, she felt another sensation she had never known before creeping up through her body.

It travelled through her breasts and into her throat until as it touched her lips she knew that this was what she had always wanted and was the love she thought she would never find.

It was wonderful, ecstatic, at the same time so surprising, and gave her a sensation of rapture that was different from anything she had ever imagined it was possible to feel.

Because her whole body quivered against him Kane's arms held her closer still, and now his lips were passionate and the wonder of it was something Octavia had never known or dreamt of.

She was not afraid but caught up in a rapture in which she seemed to be floating in the sky amongst the stars, and it was very, very wonderful.

Only when Kane raised his head did she look up at him feeling she was dazzled by the moonlight and the intensity of her feelings, and it was impossible to speak.

"How can you be so beautiful?" he asked. "To me you are the very embodiment of the treasures I have searched for, found, and longed to find more."

Then he was kissing her again, kissing her fiercely, as if he was afraid she would elude him and he would have to go on looking for her only to be disappointed.

Again sensations rising within her which were different from anything she had ever known and seemed to be part of the stars and the music she could still hear very faintly vibrating towards them.

It was so exciting, and yet so ecstatic and spiritual that when finally Kane let her go Octavia could only hide her face against his neck, while her heart beat frantically, and it was impossible to think.

"How can this have happened?" she heard Kane ask.

Raising her face to his she whispered:

"I . . . love you! I did not know that . . . love could be so . . . utterly and completely . . . wonderful!"

"That is what I want you to say," Kane replied, "but it is very much easier to kiss you."

He kissed her again until she forgot the Sphinx, the Pyramids, the stars, and everything except him.

She could only feel as if the moonlight invaded her whole body, rippled through her breasts and into her lips, and as Kane kissed her he drew her very life from her and made it his.

Finally when a century of time must have passed he said in an unsteady voice:

"I must take you home, my darling."

"I...I do not want to...leave," Octavia said. "Perhaps I...shall never...feel like...this again."

He laughed tenderly and his arms tightened around her.

"I will make you feel like this, my precious, and a great deal more," he promised, "so let us go home."

He set her free but took her hand in his and led her back over the soft sand to where a little way from them the carriage was waiting.

He helped her into it and as the horses drove off he pulled her into his arms.

She rested her head on his shoulder and sighed.

"It cannot be true," she said as if she spoke to herself, "I am dreaming...and I have never known a dream like...this before!"

"It is a dream come true," Kane said, "and I might have known when I had my first glimpse of your golden hair that fate had brought us together at the most unlikely moment and that neither of us could escape."

As she remembered how narrowly they had escaped in the train, Octavia said, the fear back in her voice:

"Be careful...you must be very careful! If anything should happen to you I, too, would want...to die!"

Kane's arms tightened around her.

"We have kissed beneath the Sphinx," he said, "and we both know there is no death."

"It is easy to . . . believe that," Octavia said, "but if I have to wait until another life to . . . find you again it will seem . . . a very, very long wait!"

Kane laughed.

"That is true, and that is why, my precious, we must make the very best of being together in this."

Then as if he wished to make sure of her he was kissing her again, kissing her as they drove from the desert onto the road which led towards Cairo, and so quickly that she was surprised, they were back at the Villa.

There was Hassam waiting to greet them at the door and to tell them that dinner would be ready as soon as they had had their baths.

As Octavia entered her bedroom she saw one of her new evening-gowns was hanging up for her to wear.

Because she wanted to look lovely for Kane, she bathed and dressed quickly, but took quite a long time in arranging her hair.

She was wondering how she should do up her gown at the back when there was a knock on the door and a young woman whom she guessed was either Hassam's wife or his eldest daughter came in and salaamed.

She could not speak English but explained in mime what she had come to do. Octavia let her fasten her gown and knew by the expression on the woman's face how much she admired her appearance.

She thanked her, knowing she would understand, and hurried down the stairs.

Kane was standing in the white Sitting-Room which was lit with oil-lamps.

He looked very dramatic wearing a white shirt and a bow tie, and instead of an evening-coat he wore a wide red silk cummerbund round his waist.

It gave him a raffish appearance, almost as if he was a pirate or a hero in some melodrama, and as Octavia stared at him he held out his arms.

She ran towards him and pulling her against him he kissed her, then holding her at arms' length he said:

"Let me look at you! I want to see you in your new finery, but I cannot imagine it could make you any lovelier than you are already."

"I am very, very thrilled to have it," Octavia replied, "but I am...afraid it must have been very...expensive."

"That is immaterial."

With what was an obvious effort he took his eyes from her face to examine her gown.

It was beautiful and exceedingly fashionable with a *décolletage* draped with white tulle which was sprinkled with silver sequins.

There was a touch of silver beneath the tulle skirt which flared out at the bottom with frill upon frill ornamented with glittering sequins.

There was a silver sash to encircle Octavia's waist which cascaded down the back of her gown, and there was a little bunch of flowers fashioned of the same tulle and glittering with *diamanté* to wear in her hair.

"Are you...pleased?" she asked anxiously.

"'Pleased' is not the right word," Kane replied, "but I will tell you about that later."

She wondered why he did not tell her now, then

thought it was because a few seconds later Hassam announced that dinner was ready.

What she ate or drank it was impossible afterwards to remember, but she knew that everything tasted like the food of the gods.

All she could think of was how handsome Kane looked, and how exciting it was to be beside him.

Even what they talked about seemed lost in the emotions he aroused in her and when his eyes rested on her lips she felt as if he kissed her.

Nevertheless, they sat for a long time in the candle-lit Dining-Room with the *punkah* moving slowly over-head and the moonlight shining in through the open windows.

Then at last Kane said:

"I think you should go to bed, my darling. It is getting late."

He came close to her as he spoke and kissed her gently.

Because instantly the moonlight within her leapt towards his lips it was impossible to argue as she wanted to do and beg him to let her stay a little longer.

Instead, because he wished it, she went up the stairs into her bedroom.

The Egyptian woman was waiting to undo her gown, and when she hung it up in the wardrobe she left the room.

Octavia put on one of her new lace-trimmed di-aphanous nightgowns, and felt it was so lovely that it was a pity Kane could not see it.

She loosened her hair until it fell over her shoulders then she got into bed.

One side of the mosquito netting was not down

and it was only when she was sitting back against the pillows with one candle alight on the table beside her that she realised she would have to get out of bed again and put it into place.

Just as she was thinking she must make the effort the door of her room opened and Kane came in.

She looked at him in surprise as he came towards her across the room wearing a long robe.

Then a sudden thought struck her and she asked quickly:

"What has . . . happened? Is anything . . . wrong?"

"No, of course not," he replied. "Everything is all right, my darling, and now I can tell you how beautiful you are and explain how much you mean to me."

For a moment Octavia just stared at him in surprise.

Then as he sat down on the side of the mattress facing her she said:

"I . . . I want you to tell me those things . . . but perhaps now there is no . . . need for it . . . you should not have . . . come to my bedroom."

"I think there is every need for it," Kane replied, "and, darling, although it may all seem to be happening rather quickly, we know we love each other, and there is no reason why I should not make you mine."

Octavia looked at him not understanding and Kane went on:

"You are not a very good liar. I knew when you told me the man who had left you in Alexandria was your brother that he was actually with you in a very different capacity. So I think it is fate that I should take his place and look after you far more adequately than he has done."

"I . . . I do not . . . know what you are saying!" Octavia exclaimed.

"Then let me make it a little clearer," Kane said. "You will be mine and I will love you, protect you and you need never be afraid of being alone again."

It was what Octavia wanted to hear. At the same time there was something wrong about it.

As she looked at him questioningly he bent forward to put his arms around her, but she pushed herself back against the pillows and held him off by pressing her hands against his chest.

"I . . . I still do not . . . understand."

"Is there any need for words?" Kane asked. "Your lover left you, and he therefore cannot have loved you as he should have done. But I promise you, if nothing else, I would never leave you alone, with only £25 between you and starvation!"

Suddenly Octavia understood, and as Kane would have held her closer she struggled violently against him.

"How can you . . . think such . . . things?" she asked. "How could you . . . believe that . . . Tony was my . . . lover? He is my brother . . . I told you that he is . . . my brother!"

"You expect me to believe that?"

Now Kane spoke in a rather different voice and there was a sharp note in it that had not been there before.

"It is true! It is true!" Octavia cried. "Tony is my brother, and he only left me because he . . . wanted to be with the girl he . . . wishes to marry and he had no room on her yacht for me."

Kane took his arms from Octavia and sat back.

"Are you telling me the truth?"

"Of course I am telling you . . . the truth!" Octavia explained. "How can you imagine that I would . . . do anything so . . . wrong . . . so wicked as to . . . have a . . . lover?"

She found it difficult to say the word.

It seemed so humiliating that Kane should think such things of her that the colour flared in her face and her eyes filled with tears.

Then in a broken little voice she said:

"I . . . I was frightened of . . . going back to England . . . alone because there were . . . men on the ship coming out who . . . looked at me in a . . . horrid way! But because Tony was with me then I did not . . . think about them . . . but it might have been . . . different if I had been alone."

Still Kane did not speak, but just sat staring at her as she went on:

"I . . . trusted you . . . I did not think that . . . you were like them . . . or would think of me as doing . . . anything so . . . wicked!"

Now the tears overflowed and ran down her cheeks.

"You are telling me seriously that Tony is your brother?" Kane asked, and his voice seemed to come from a very long way away.

"Of course he is my brother! And the reason why he brought me with him to find the American girl he wants to marry was that it was . . . impossible for us to stay any longer at . . . home!"

She gave a little sob before she went on:

"He told me that he would arrange when we got

123

to Cairo...which was...where he thought...she was going...that there would be...people to...look after me."

"People?" Kane repeated.

"I think to be honest," Octavia said in a small voice, "that he meant...men...and he thought... because we have no money I should...try to get m— married!"

She felt Kane stiffen and because it sounded so fast and unladylike she added:

"But I was...determined I would not...marry any man...unless I...loved him."

Kane got up from the bed and walked towards the window.

Octavia thinking he was going to leave her said:

"Please...understand...please...please understand...and I know you must...despise me...but there was...nothing else I could do...except agree to what Tony wanted."

"So you thought," Kane said almost sharply, "as a large number of English girls have thought before, that there are a great many in Cairo who are prospective husbands!"

There was a scathing note in his voice that sounded like a whip-lash.

Because she knew what he was feeling for her, Octavia's tears poured down her face and she lowered her head so that he should not see them.

"I...I am sorry," she said, "sorry if you think I have...deceived you...but I...never expected you to...feel like this about me."

"I did not expect it myself," Kane replied, "but I still do not understand seeing how young and inexperienced you are, how your brother could have done anything so callous, so utterly disgraceful as to leave you alone in a place like Alexandria."

"He thought . . . I would . . . go straight . . . home."

"I can think of a great number of reasons why that might have proved impossible, apart from the fact that quite by chance I came into your bedroom!"

"I . . . I was frightened . . . but then I was sure I could . . . trust you."

"I am a man," Kane said, "and you are very beautiful, Octavia!"

"Nobody has ever . . . told me that . . . before, and . . . perhaps Tony did not realise it would . . . get me into trouble."

"I imagine your brother was thinking of himself, and not of you!" Kane said scathingly.

Because she could not bear him to disparage Tony and speak in that hard, contemptuous voice Octavia said quickly:

"Tony is really very . . . kind and he does . . . think about me, but he has no money and no . . . chance of . . . ever making any, and he loves Virginia for . . . herself beside the fact that she is . . . very rich."

She felt as she spoke that she was making the whole situation worse, and yet it was true, and she did not wish to lie to Kane.

At the same time she thought it would be a great mistake to tell him who she really was or that they had done anything so wrong as to run away when her father had just died.

She felt he would also have been shocked that she had not insisted on him buying her black gowns instead of such pretty ones.

The more she thought about herself and Tony, the more complicated the whole story seemed to grow, and the more impossible to explain to anybody without it appearing even more reprehensible than it was already.

Kane was staring out into the darkness and she could see the stars in the sky and felt as if he was as far away from her as they were.

"Please...please," she said pleadingly, "do not be...angry with me."

Then because she felt she had lost him completely she added brokenly:

"I will...go away tomorrow...if that is what you...want me to do."

He turned round from the window.

"And where would you go? Do you really want to travel back alone to England?"

"Of course I do not want to go back...I want to stay with you...but you are angry with me...and although I want to please you...I know Mama would be...shocked at what you have...suggested."

He did not speak or move and after a moment she whispered:

"I do not...really know what happens when a man makes...love to a woman, because Mama never told me...and after she died I had...nobody to ask. I think it would be very...very wonderful if I felt like I did...when you...kissed me...but...it would still be wrong...at least...that is what I have always believed."

She was thinking as she spoke how sometimes the women who worked in the house had spoken with horror of some poor girl who had, as they described it, 'got into trouble.'

Octavia had not been certain what this meant, except that one girl had had a baby by a married man and had been so unhappy about it that she had drowned herself in the river.

But instead of being distressed by what had happened to her, some of the older women had even said it was 'the only decent thing' she could have done.

Because Octavia had been quite young when it happened she had not thought about it for long.

Now it all came back to her and she could remember how they had despised the girl and the unkind way they had condemned her for what she had done.

Kane walked back to the bed and sat down again where he had been before, facing her.

He looked at her for a long time, at the tears on her cheeks and eye-lashes, and her eyes dark and frightened as they looked at him while her lips trembled.

He sat there saying nothing until in a hesitating little voice Octavia said:

"I . . . I . . . am . . . sorry . . . please . . . please . . . forgive me."

"There is nothing to forgive. It is just that I misunderstood what had happened to you, and perhaps for the first time in my life made a complete error judgment for which I can only blame myself."

"Then . . . you do not . . . want me to go . . . away?"

"No! Of course not!" he said sharply. "You will stay here until I decide what I can do about you."

"You are still very . . . angry with me?"

"Not angry with you, but with your brother, and as it happens, with myself!"

She gave a little sigh of relief, but her eyes were still troubled as she said in a voice he could hardly hear:

"But you . . . do not . . . love me . . . any more?"

"Of course I love you!" Kane replied. "I love you and I want you. But Octavia, I must be frank and tell you that the life I lead, which is a very complicated one at the moment and very undesirable from a woman's point of view, makes it impossible for me to be married."

"But you . . . pretended I was your . . . wife!"

It was such a child-like remark that Kane could not help smiling.

"I asked you to pretend to be my wife to save my life, but that was rather different."

It flashed through Octavia's mind that it would be very wonderful to be his wife.

Then she saw it was something she wanted more than anything else in the whole world, but he did not want her, and there was nothing she could do about it.

As if he knew what she was thinking, Kane said:

"Do not be unhappy, Octavia. Go to sleep, and we will talk about this again in the morning. Now I have to do a lot of hard thinking as to the best solution for both of us."

As he spoke he bent forward, pressed her back against the pillows and kissed her on the forehead.

"Go to sleep," he said quietly, "and think of what you felt when you looked at the Pyramids and I kissed you under the Sphinx."

"I shall be thinking . . . of you," Octavia whispered.

She thought he had not heard as he rose, stepped back, lowered the mosquito net from the top of the bed, and blew out the candle.

He walked across the room, and without looking back at her shut the door behind him.

chapter six

OCTAVIA cried herself to sleep and when Hassam brought her breakfast in the morning her eyes were heavy and her head ached.

However, after she had drunk her coffee she felt a little better and wondered if Kane was thinking about her as she was thinking about him, and what he was planning for the day.

When Hassam came back to fetch her breakfast-tray he said:

"Master out, not come back 'til afternoon."

"He will not be back for luncheon?" Octavia asked.

Hassam shook his head.

"Think not."

Octavia felt her disappointment was almost unbearable.

All through the night she had longed to go to Kane

and tell him that she loved him and beg him to go on loving her.

She knew it would be a very wrong and reprehensible thing for her to do, but she felt as if he had taken away with him all the rapture she had felt when he kissed her by the Sphinx.

Now it had gone she would never find it again.

She lay in bed for a long time, feeling miserable and fighting against the tears which kept coming into her eyes.

Then she told herself she was being ridiculous, and when Kane returned the last thing he would want to see was an unhappy face distorted by tears.

"Women weep and wail to get their own way," her father had said once. "What a man wants is for a woman to smile, laugh and make him feel happy."

She had been quite small and sitting on his knee when he said this.

He had talked as if he was annoyed over something which had just happened to him.

It was only when she grew older that Octavia realised that because her father was so handsome and so dashing he left many broken hearts behind him.

Sometimes when piles of letters in feminine handwriting had come by post, she had known by the way her father thrust them aside that however much the ladies he had discarded pleaded with him he had no longer any interest in them.

She told herself the best thing she could do now would be to go away.

Whatever Kane might say, she was obviously an encumbrance, and as she loved him she knew it would be difficult not to cling to him and be upset if he did not respond.

"How can he make me feel as I did when he kissed me," she asked, "and then not want me any more?"

It was a question women had asked themselves since the beginning of time and for which there was no answer.

But while Octavia knew it would crucify her to leave Kane and Cairo behind, she thought it might be worse to stay and suffer the tortures of hell because she loved him and yet could not do what he wanted her to do.

Now that she could think about it quietly, she could remember being shocked when Tony had told her about the women who amused her father.

Although she had not really understood what he was talking about, she knew now her father had made love to them.

They had been his mistresses, but according to Tony they had never lasted very long.

While they cried and bewailed their broken hearts, her father went away looking elsewhere for amusement, and invariably that meant another beautiful woman.

"How could I be like them?" Octavia asked. "How could I ever say my . . . prayers if I was . . . doing what Mama would consider a . . . sin, and so would . . . the Church?"

Every Sunday at home she had gone to the little Church in the village which had been built some time after the monks had been turned out of the Priory.

It meant a long walk there and a long walk back.

But she had prayed that her father would not spend all the money in London that was needed to repair the house and pay the wages of the people who worked for him.

She also prayed that someday they would be together as a family and be happy again.

She felt that would be impossible without her mother, and yet when her father did come home and Tony was there too they would laugh and forget the leaking roof and the empty spaces in the rooms which showed that things had been sold.

'Perhaps one day I shall have children of my own,' Octavia thought. 'But how could I ever be happy if I knew I had done something wrong and wicked, and that if they knew of it they would be ashamed of me?"

It was a question for which she felt there was only one answer: she must leave Kane and go back to England.

Even to think of it made her feel helpless, and she had no idea how she could find out the times of the trains which would carry her to Alexandria and the ships which would be sailing from the port.

She knew she would not be able to afford one of the P. & O. Liners, and yet she shrank from the idea of travelling in the same sort of ship in which she and Tony had come from Tilbury.

"What can I . . . do? What . . . can I do?" she asked despairingly, and felt that only Kane could give her the right answer.

She got up and dressed herself, then went downstairs to sit on the verandah.

She ate a lonely luncheon in the Dining-Room and

although it was well cooked and delicious she could not eat more than a mouthful of any of the dishes.

Then she went back out onto the verandah again wondering what Kane was doing, and if he was deliberately staying away because he was angry with her.

Hassam came in carrying a newspaper and set it down beside her.

"English newspapers, Missie," he said, "only five days old. Come quick!"

"How do they manage to arrive so quickly?" Octavia asked.

"Lord Cromer arrange," Hassam replied. "Come train to Marseilles, then ship Alexandria, then Cairo."

Hassam spoke as if it was something he had learned by heart, and Octavia could not help laughing.

When he had gone away she picked up '*The Morning Post*,' knowing that her father's death would have been reported in one edition of some days before and that she would have missed it.

She turned over the pages not taking much interest in the plans for the Queen's Diamond Jubilee which was to take place next year, the difficulties which had arisen in India, or a long article about the Gold Fields on the Klondike.

Suddenly a paragraph lower down the page caught her attention and she read:

FANTASTIC FIND
IN ANCIENT PRIORY IN KENT

Following the report which was published last week of the fourth Lord Birkenhall's death at his home, an ancient Priory in the village of Meadowfields in Kent, Art Dealers have discovered amongst the family collection a picture painted by Holbein, which is of great interest to connoisseurs of Art.

It had been thought for centuries that the picture was a portrait of General Birke who originally received the Priory and its lands as a reward for his Services after King Henry VIII's Dissolution of the Monasteries.

It now appears that the portrait in question, which needs some restoration, was painted by Holbein, and is of the last Prior who lived in the Priory.

It seemed a mystery why such a famous artist should have been commissioned to paint him until those who were investigating the portrait discovered that the very heavy and ornate frame in which he is displayed is made of solid gold.

The British Portrait Gallery which is interested in acquiring the portrait, believes that the Abbott had prior knowledge that the King intended to seize the Priory and saved much of its wealth by having it converted into gold.

This was then made into a frame which it was thought must have been hung in an inconspicuous place in order to avoid detection.

Since then generations of Birkes have had their portraits painted and these, like the house itself and most of the estate, are entailed onto the heir to the Baronecy.

The new and fifth Lord Birkenhall is at the moment somewhere abroad and every effort is *being made by his Solicitors to get in touch with him, to inform him of this sensational and exciting discovery.*

Octavia read the paragraphs not once, but three times to be quite certain she had not misunderstood what she read.

Then as she felt stunned by the news, she also felt with a leap of her heart that her prayers had been answered.

Now Tony could return home and not only could restore the Priory but could afford to live there without being dependent on Virginia or anybody else's money.

The picture of the Prior, because it was not a portrait of one of their ancestors, could be sold and so could the frame.

It seemed incredible and Octavia thought it was a gift from God which she had not expected.

"Thank You, God, thank You!" she said in her heart, then wondered how she could get in touch with Tony.

She was sure as she thought about it that Kane would know a way by which they could communicate with Virginia's yacht if it was now at Constantinople.

Tony would then be able to return home and no longer be ashamed to meet those to whom their father owed so much money.

"Thank You, thank You," she whispered again and her gratitude seemed to fly up into the sky.

Then, in case she had made a mistake she read the report again.

As she waited for Kane's return she felt the minutes seem to creep by, and yet at the same time, she was so excited that she no longer felt unhappy.

There was however, a hard little lump in her heart when she remembered he did not love her as she loved him.

Then she began to wonder frantically if anything had happened to him, and if those who were trying to kill him had perhaps succeeded.

Hassam came to find her as she was walking in the garden feeling it was impossible to sit still.

"Message from Master," he said as he reached her.

"What is it?" Octavia enquired.

"Master say sorry away so long. Very busy."

Octavia wanted to know what he was doing, but it was no use asking Hassam and the servant went on:

"Master say dinner-party tonight. Very smart. Missie be ready seven o'clock. He back time to dress."

Octavia gave a sigh.

It did not sound as if there would be any time to talk to Kane or explain to him who she was and show him the paragraphs in the newspaper.

She wanted to go to the dinner-party with him but she had the feeling it was something to do with his work. He would therefore not be particularly interested in her except that he needed her to accompany him and pretend to be his wife.

She did not know how she knew this, she just sensed it, and she went indoors and up to her bedroom to decide which of her beautiful new gowns she would wear.

She thought at first it was a pity she had worn the white and silver one the night before.

Then she found there was one even lovelier, but

when she looked at it it made her think that it was rather like a bridal gown.

Since that was something she would never wear for Kane, it was obviously inappropriate.

The other two gowns were more simple and she knew that if, as Hassam had said, it was to be a smart party, she must do as he wished and look her best.

She waited downstairs for a long time, then she had her bath, and although she spent ages arranging her hair in the mirror she was sure he had not yet returned to the villa.

Just as she was beginning to think he might be late and perhaps would not be able to come after all, she heard a carriage drive up to the front door and knew he had returned.

She felt her heart leap and she longed to run down to greet him, but as she was only wearing her petticoat that was impossible.

She heard him coming running up the stairs, calling for Hassam as he did so, and go into his bedroom to slam the door behind him.

She looked at the clock and realised that he had less than a quarter-of-an-hour to bathe and dress, and that meant that she too must be ready and not keep him waiting.

The woman who had attended her before must have realised she would be needed because she came into the room and lifted up the white gown which Octavia had laid on the bed.

When she had put it on, Octavia realised how skilfully it was made and in its way almost sensational.

Of white crepe, it had puffed sleeves of real lace

ornamented with *diamanté,* which also glittered round the *décolletage.*

The same stones sparkled like dew-drops on the gown, and on the frills which edged the hem, drifting away into a small train at the back which glistened with every movement.

The whole effect was to make Octavia twinkle as if she was a star.

There were long white kid-gloves for her to wear and a small bag to carry which matched the gown.

To wear over it there was a long white chiffon scarf that was also embroidered with *diamanté.*

Holding her bag and with the scarf in her hand Octavia took a last look at herself in the mirror, then walked slowly down the stairs.

She was standing waiting for Kane when he came into the Sitting-Room, and while she was hoping he would admire her she gasped at how magnificent he looked.

It was a long time since she had seen her father in full evening-dress, but Kane was not only wearing a stiff white shirt and white tie, but his long-tailed evening-coat was decorated with medals and stars.

Around his neck a medal in the shape of a cross, hung from a coloured ribbon.

It was not only his appearance which made her feel tongue-tied, but the fact that he was there so that her love for him seemed to well up inside her like a tidal wave.

She wanted, as she had never wanted anything in her life before, to run into his arms and that he should kiss her.

Instead he walked quickly across the room to stand

beside her and say in a low voice:

"Listen, Octavia, this is very important!"

She raised her eyes to his and he went on:

"I could not get back before to tell you that tonight we are dining with Lord Cromer and it is absolutely essential that you help me by playing the part, as you have done so effectively before, of my wife."

Octavia did not speak and Kane said with a twisted smile:

"—a very beautiful one, of whom I am justly proud, and we have only recently been married and are still on our honeymoon."

Octavia remembering how he had said last night that he could not marry because of his work, could not look straight at him, but fixed her eyes on the decoration at his neck as he went on:

"We will not be announced as Mr. and Mrs. Gordon."

She looked puzzled, but she did not speak and Kane continued:

"Now we are Lord and Lady Stratheagle, and as far as the principal guest is concerned, we have just arrived in Egypt."

The way he said 'principal guest' made Octavia look up at him questioningly, and he said:

"He is a man called Abul Pasha, and Lord Cromer is giving the dinner especially in his honour."

Instinctively Octavia knew there was some special reason for this and she asked:

"Is Abul Pasha the man whom you suspect is behind the pending revolution and who needs the money from the tomb you have found?"

"That is quick of you," Kane said approvingly,

"but the truth is, while we are suspicious of his intentions, we have nothing concrete to go on."

"And he does not know who you are?" Octavia asked.

"If he is the man we suspect he is, he has told his followers to destroy Kane Gordon. Therefore it is essential for me to be presented to him this evening as someone very different."

"I can... understand that!" Octavia said, "but it... may be... dangerous."

"We are safe enough in the presence of Lord Cromer," Kane promised, "and I can assure you he will be protected in every possible way from anything that might happen to him."

"Is it... wise to invite... this man into... his house?"

"We are hoping he may give us a lead by something he says, or something he does. We are working in the dark, and that is why I want you to keep your wits about you and tell me afterwards if you see or hear anything suspicious."

"You know I... will do... that," Octavia replied, "but I am... frightened for... you."

Kane smiled and she thought for the first time there was a tenderness in his eyes that had not been there while he had been talking.

Then he said quickly:

"We must go! It would be a mistake to arrive late. Be very careful what you say to me. In Egypt not only the walls have ears, but the air itself!"

She picked up the scarf she had laid on a chair and Kane put it over her shoulders.

She thought that for a moment his hands lingered as if he wanted to touch her.

Then as if he told himself he was on duty, he said

in the brisk, authoritative voice that she knew so well:

"Get into the carriage. We have not far to go."

She lifted the short train at the back of her gown and did as she was told.

Only when they were sitting close together on the comfortable padded seat of the closed carriage did Kane reach out and take her gloved hand in his.

"I am sorry, you have had to be alone for so long today," he said gently, "but it was impossible for me to come to you as I wished to do."

"I . . . I thought perhaps you had . . . forgotten me."

She felt his fingers tighten on hers.

"I did not do that, but tonight I have to think, not of any danger to myself or to you, but to Lord Cromer and if anything should happen to him, to Egypt."

"Surely it is not . . . possible for him to be . . . killed in his own house?" Octavia asked in horror.

"No, of course not," Kane said soothingly, "and we do not even know if Abul Pasha is behind the incidents which have aroused our suspicions. Nevertheless, we are aware there is a great deal of seething sedition building up secretly and there is still no sign of Manton."

He spoke the last sentence in so low a voice that Octavia could hardly hear what he said.

Although it was impossible for the men driving the carriage to overhear what they were saying, she was aware that Kane was really afraid that their disguise might be penetrated.

"Lady Stratheagle!" Octavia exclaimed. "It is a very pretty title."

"That is what I thought," Kane agreed, "and it suits you."

It flashed through Octavia's mind that any name

she was called which meant she was Kane's wife would seem like the sound of trumpets, or the music of the spheres.

Then she felt her spirits drop as she knew he had no intention of marrying her. As she had told herself even before she read about the find at the Priory, she knew she must leave him and go away.

'I will talk to him about it tomorrow,' she thought.

Then even though he appeared to be relaxed she realised he was tense, and fearful of the dangers that lay ahead of him, and she started to pray for his safety.

* * *

If the house in which they were dining was a surprise, so was their host.

Kane had not explained that Lord Cromer, as the great man of Egypt who was in effect its uncrowned and unacclaimed King, was living in the very modest Palace which before his arrival was simply the British Consulate.

Outside the pillars at the front drive and along the verandah were impressive but inside Octavia thought, it was like a large comfortable English country house.

She had expected Lord Cromer to be a regal figure.

Instead she found he was a ruddy-faced man with short white hair, a trim moustache, wearing gold-rimmed spectacles.

He looked something like a Surgeon or perhaps a reliable family Solicitor.

Yet because she was perceptive Octavia could feel the vibrations that came from him were strong and authoritative.

In fact they were so commanding, that she could

understand why Kane was tremendously impressed by him, and that without contradiction in Egypt his word was law.

Lady Cromer received them against a background of exquisite flowers which Octavia learnt was her main personal interest and to which she devoted every moment she could spare from her official duties.

There were a number of other people already present, and as Kane and Octavia were introduced to them as Lord and Lady Stratheagle she was aware that they were all high ranking Army Officers.

All of them, with perhaps the exception of two *Aides-de-Camp*, were older than Kane.

If they had known him before or recognised him as Kane Gordon, they made no sign of it, but merely expressed politely how pleased they were to meet him and his wife.

Then they made desultory conversation about the weather and various events of social interest taking place in Cairo.

Four or five minutes late, as if to show his importance, Abul Pasha arrived.

Kane had deliberately moved with Octavia beside him to the open window of the long Drawing-Room from which he could see the front of the house.

They could both watch the open carriage driven by a gaudily dressed coachman, with a footman beside him, draw up at the front door.

Sitting on the back seat was the man they were waiting to meet, and opposite him were two of his servants wearing traditional white livery, in their case ornamented with green, and on their heads were green turbans.

Octavia had noticed on arrival that Lord Cromer's

resident servants were in white, but with red facings and red turbans.

She had the idea, and meant to ask Kane about it later, that it was the same way the servants were dressed in every British Embassy abroad and in Government Houses in India.

She wondered, as she watched Abul Pasha step out of the carriage, whether he had deliberately copied the British in dressing his servants in an almost identical manner.

Then she remembered that in the East green was almost a sacred colour, since a green turban usually indicated that its wearer had visited Mecca.

It was impossible to ask all the questions that surged into her mind before Kane turned away from the window and started a conversation with an elderly General.

He had a magnificent display of medals to show for the long years of his service in the British Army.

His *Aide-de-Camp* came into the room to announce:

"His Excellency Abul Pasha, My Lord!"

As the man they were waiting for walked into the room, Octavia saw he was not very tall, but slim and wiry, and immaculately dressed in a native coat decorated with silver thread.

Lord and Lady Cromer greeted him effusively.

Then as Lord Cromer took him around the assembled throng, introducing each of his guests, Octavia was vividly aware even before she spoke to Abul Pasha that he was evil.

She could feel it emanating from him, see it in his dark eyes, and knew that everything Kane suspected about him was true.

146

As Lord Cromer reached them he said:

"Now I want Your Excellency to meet two of my guests who have just arrived from England, and as it happens, are a bride and bridegroom—Lord and Lady Stratheagle!"

Abul Pasha held out his hand and as Octavia took it she felt as if she touched a snake.

Then without speaking to her he turned towards Kane.

"I hope you, My Lord, will enjoy your stay in Cairo," he said.

"We certainly hope to," Kane replied in the lofty, indifferent tone of the Englishman abroad, "and we also hope it will not become too hot!"

"I think you are fairly safe for the next week or two," Abul Pasha replied.

Then as Lord Cromer drew him away to meet two other guests, Octavia felt she wanted to scream aloud that he was dangerous and he should be imprisoned before he could create any more trouble.

She knew now for certain that it was he who had sent the two men to kill Kane.

Yet she thought despairingly it might be something they could never prove, and he would go on plotting and planning against Lord Cromer and the British Rule in Egypt.

And perhaps his revolution would be successful as Arabi Pasha's had failed.

Then as Lord Cromer finished his introductions dinner was announced and they moved into the high-ceilinged, brightly-lit Dining-Room where the servants in their white and red livery stood behind every chair.

But not behind one, for Octavia saw in surprise

147

that there were two men with green turbans standing on either side of the chair in which Abul Pasha was to be seated.

Lord and Lady Cromer must have been aware of it, although they appeared not to notice. But Octavia could not help thinking it was an insult not only to Pasha's hosts, but also to the British.

As they sat down at the table, Octavia realised that there were many more men than women.

In fact she found that while she was sitting on Lord Cromer's left, Abul Pasha was on his right and Kane was on the other side of the Egyptian.

The few other women present were dotted amongst the men almost like flowers, to brighten the severity of their evening-clothes.

Octavia was the only woman who was not wearing a tiara, and she thought Kane had been remiss in not providing her with one, even if it was only borrowed for the occasion.

She was glad that the *diamanté* on her gown sparkled, and that she had at the last moment fixed a white orchid in her hair because she thought it gave her a little height.

Lord Cromer engaged her in conversation and they talked about the Pyramids, the progress of the Aswan Dam, and whether she would like to meet the Princess Nadi Fazir, who was a cousin of the Khedive.

It was the sort of conversation which she could imagine any Englishwoman might have in any part of the world if she found herself at a dinner-party at a British Embassy.

It all sounded so easy, so glib and so unaffected.

She could hear Kane telling Abul Pasha some

amusing things that had happened to them on their journey from England and making him laugh.

She thought no actors could have played their parts more brilliantly than they were managing to do.

She was aware that Lord Cromer deliberately did not ask her any embarrassing questions about where she came from in England, or their recent marriage.

She felt that if everybody else in the party was deceived by Kane's assumed title, Lord Cromer knew his real identity.

Octavia could see that Kane was getting on very well with Abul Pasha, and she longed to warn him that the man was dangerous.

She found herself thinking of him as a cobra rising up ready to strike with its forked tongue and kill.

She felt herself shiver and the General on her other side asked:

"I cannot believe you are cold, Lady Stratheagle, or are you feeling a draught from the *punkahs* over-head?"

Octavia smiled.

"I was shuddering at my thoughts," she said, "or perhaps, as my Nanny used to say, there is a ghost walking over my grave!"

The General laughed.

"I have a feeling my Nanny said the same thing, but it is something which happens to all of us at some time or another."

"But of course it should not happen in this climate," Octavia said lightly. "I found it very warm this after-noon, even though I was doing nothing more arduous than sitting on a comfortable verandah."

After that the conversation seemed so banal that

she thought she would have yawned at it herself if she had not been listening all the time to what Kane was saying and her eyes were drawn irresistibly to Abul Pasha.

She felt as if the dinner dragged on interminably until at last Lady Cromer rose and the ladies left the Dining-Room leaving the men to their port.

"I am sure you would like to come upstairs, Lady Stratheagle," Lady Cromer said, "and I want to show you in my bedroom some new orchids I have just bred, which I think are beautiful."

She led the way and Octavia agreed that the orchids were very lovely and quite different from any she had ever seen before.

As she had never seen an orchid before coming to Egypt and then in the garden of the Villa, she could hardly speak from experience. But all Lady Cromer wanted her to do was to eulogise over her flowers and that was easy.

The ladies chatted, tidied their hair in the long mirrors, then went down the stairs to the Drawing-Room.

Octavia was coming down behind the others, and only as she reached the door did she realise that she had left the little bag which matched her gown upstairs on Lady Croner's dressing-table.

Without making any explanation she hurried back up the stairs and along the passage which led to Lady Cromer's bedroom.

She had almost reached it when a door opened and a servant came out of an adjoining room.

He started when he saw her, then made a very low

bow, in fact so low that she looked at him in surprise.

Then she realised he was wearing a green turban.

It struck her as strange that one of Abul Pasha's servants should be upstairs in the house.

Still bowing his head the man hurried away in such a strange and surreptitious manner that Octavia stared after him in surprise.

He was carrying something in his hand and just as he reached the end of the corridor and disappeared, she realised that before he bowed in front of her she had noticed, almost without being aware of it, that he had a scar beneath his left eye.

She stood very still, realising it was the man who had been sent to kill Kane and she knew at the same time what he had been holding in his hand.

For a moment the enormity of it swept over her so that she felt it hard to breathe.

Then almost as if Kane was directing her what to do, she went without hurrying into Lady Cromer's bedroom, picked up her small bag from the dressing-table, and walked down the stairs again.

The ladies were chatting in the Drawing-Room as she joined them, and she explained to Lady Cromer where she had been.

"Such a pretty bag!" Lady Cromer exclaimed. "I am quite sorry that you remembered it!"

"It is indeed," another lady said, "and so clever to have a bag to match your gown! I must make sure I do the same when I am extravagant enough to buy such a beautiful gown as yours!"

"You are very kind," Octavia smiled.

They chatted away until with a sudden constriction

of her heart Octavia heard voices and realised that the gentlemen led by Lord Cromer were coming into the Drawing-Room.

Abul Pasha was talking animatedly to his host and Octavia deliberately moved towards the far end of the room so that she would not be seated beside him, at least until she had been able to speak to Kane.

It was difficult to manoeuvre her way to his side without it appearing obvious, but somehow she managed it.

He was deep in conversation with one of the young *Aides-de-Camp* who was explaining as she reached them some difficult exercise they had undertaken the previous day in the desert.

She waited until there was a pause, then she said to Kane:

"Forgive me, darling, but I came without a handkerchief, and I wondered if I could borrow yours?"

She knew by the expression in Kane's eyes that his quick brain told him she had something to say to him.

As he felt in his pocket for a handkerchief he managed by what seemed a completely natural movement to insert himself between Octavia and the *Aide-de-Camp*.

"Thank you," Octavia said smiling up at him.

Then softly in a whisper that only he could hear she said:

"The man who tried to kill you has put a scorpion in our host's bedroom!"

She spoke quickly, half-afraid because her voice was so soft that Kane would not hear what she said.

But as she finished speaking she was aware that he understood, and he said:

"Here is my handkerchief, and fortunately it is a clean one."

"Thank you, darling, and I hope you will not want it back!"

She gave him an enticing smile and deliberately moved away from him across the room, as if she wished to look at some attractive *objets d'art* on a table which also contained a number of silver-framed photographs.

"How many delightful things they have in this house!" she said to a man who was standing beside the table.

"That is what I think every time I come here," he answered.

As he spoke Octavia was able to look around and she realised that Kane and the *Aide-de-Camp* had left the room.

Only then did a sudden sharp fear creep into her mind that she might have sent Kane to his death.

Supposing, she asked herself, that when he reached the bedroom he searched for the scorpion and it killed him?

He had already told her that a scorpion moved very fast and when it struck there was no escape.

She could imagine Kane hurriedly looking for the small insect in a large bedroom and suddenly finding himself the victim instead of Lord Cromer for whom it was intended.

She realised that it was much easier to find a man than something small but deadly, and she wanted to scream out that Kane was in danger and send everyone in the room to help him.

Then she knew that Kane was well aware of how dangerous scorpions could be, as he had said when he showed her his collection of boxes.

Almost as if she sought for some source of comfort she knew that it must have been fate that had made her aware of what the Pasha's servant carried in his hands, and it was only because Kane had a collection of such boxes that she had learnt about them.

She remembered once many years ago her mother saying:

"Nothing is lost and nothing is ever useless in this world. We learn about something, then find to our surprise that later on it fits in like a jig-saw puzzle and completes in a different way from what we ever expected, a pattern that has been worrying us."

That, Octavia thought, was exactly what had happened now.

She had known, although she had only had a quick glimpse of it, exactly what the servant with the scar under his eye was carrying in his hands and why he had been in Lord Cromer's room.

At the same time, however much her intelligence told her that Kane could take care of himself, every nerve in her body was tense, and once again she was praying frantically that he would be safe and she would not lose him.

A little later Lady Cromer asked her to come to talk to Abul Pasha.

"He told me how much he enjoyed talking to your husband at dinner," she said, "and now he must have the pleasure of conversing with you."

Octavia sat down beside the Pasha feeling as if she had been taken into a lion's den.

"What made you come to Egypt for your honeymoon?" the Pasha asked.

He spoke extremely good English, but with an accent that made him sometimes hard to follow.

"The answer is easy," Octavia replied. "I wanted to see the Pyramids and I hope my husband will take me on a steamer up the Nile."

"You will find it a very enjoyable trip."

"I only wish I could do it in style, as Cleopatra did," Octavia smiled, "in a beautiful barge with scented sails, but I am afraid it would take too long."

"Could any journey be too long for a man on his honeymoon with you?" Abul Pasha asked.

Because she was afraid of him she thought the expression in his eyes was insulting.

Yet she knew it would be a mistake to look round the room for Kane, which might make Abul Pasha realise he was not there.

She found herself again wondering frantically if she had sent Kane into danger but she had not missed when they arrived, seeing the British sentries at the gates and outside the front door.

This assured her that Lord Cromer was very competently guarded tonight, for there would be other soldiers in the house while Abul Pasha had only three men and his coachman with him.

"I had always heard that Englishwomen were beautiful," he was saying, "and now I have seen you, Lady Stratheagle, I know my informants spoke the truth!"

He was flirting with her and Octavia with difficulty managed to reply lightly:

"Thank you for such a nice compliment, but Egypt was famous for its beautiful women when we in England were still wearing woad!"

"You would look beautiful in woad, or in anything else," Abul Pasha replied.

As he spoke the door opened and Kane came in.

An *Aide-de-Camp* was walking beside him and behind them were two other Officers in uniform, each of them carrying a pistol in his hand.

There was a sudden silence in the room as Kane walked across to where Abul Pasha was sitting and said in a quiet voice, which seemed somehow to fill the room:

"Abul Pasha, in the name of Her Majesty Queen Victoria, Empress of India, you are charged with conspiring to kill Her Majesty's representative the Consul-General of Great Britain, Lord Cromer!"

Most of the guests seemed to gasp audibly, but Abul Pasha sat very still and did not move, his dark eyes on Kane's face.

Then before he could speak Kane continued:

"Your servant has confessed to us that you ordered him to put a scorpion in Lord Cromer's room and your other servants too, who were all implicated in the plot, have been taken into detention. I must ask you to accompany these officers to where you will be detained until you are brought to trial. Every facility will be granted to you to have legal Representation."

As Kane finished speaking everybody in the room seemed to have been turned to stone.

Then as Abul Pasha rose to his feet the two officers behind Kane stepped forward to walk on each side of him.

As they did so, with a movement so swift that although Kane put out his hand to stop him, it was too late, Abul Pasha drew a knife from the pocket of his embroidered coat and plunged it into his own chest.

For a moment he stood straight and still, as if nothing had happened, only the hilt of the knife protruding from between the outside of his ribs.

Before he could fall to the ground the two officers on either side of him lifted him up by his elbows and carried him from the room, while Kane with the *Aides-de-Camp* following closed the door behind them.

After they had gone there was the sound of a deep sigh that seemed to come from everybody's lips.

Then Lord Cromer walked towards Octavia and taking her hand in his said:

"Thank you! You and your husband gave a magnificent performance for which I shall always be eternally grateful."

Then before he could say any more the Generals were round him, one of them saying:

"Now we know who was at the bottom of all the trouble, and we can only thank God he has killed himself! It will make things very much easier!"

It was Lady Cromer in a shocked tone who asked the question Octavia was dreading.

"But who found out, Evelyn, that they had put a scorpion in your room? It makes me shudder to think of it!"

She waited for an answer and Octavia said haltingly:

"I . . . I saw a servant wearing a . . . green turban coming through the door when I . . . went back to fetch my bag."

"And you saw he was one of Abul Pasha's servants! But how did you know it was a scorpion he had hidden there?" Lord Croner enquired.

"He was carrying a...box in his hand which I...recognised as being...like those used by the...Egyptians for such...dangerous insects," Octavia replied.

Then feeling embarrassed at the attention she was receiving, she saw with a lift of her heart the door open and Kane come back into the Drawing-Room.

He walked across to her and put his arm through hers.

"I might have known that you would find the answer to all our problems," he said quietly.

"He is dead?" Lord Cromer asked in his crisp, dry voice.

"He was already dead when he left this room," Kane replied, "and now, My Lord, if you will excuse us, I think I should take my wife home. She has been through enough for one night."

"She has indeed!" Lord Cromer agreed. "I can only say Lady Stratheagle, what a deep debt of gratitude I owe you personally, and I shall inform Her Majesty of the magnificent way in which you have served the Crown."

"Thank...you," Octavia said a little incoherently.

Then before she had to say any more Kane was taking her away.

Only when they were outside the room could she hear a buzz of excited voices growing higher and higher.

chapter seven

As Kane took Octavia out of the Drawing-Room and into the hall, she was not surprised to see a number of soldiers and their officers on duty.

Kane however took her quickly towards the front door and only as they stood under the portico waiting for their carriage to come up to the red carpet did she feel as if the world was beginning to swim round her and put out her hand as if to hold onto him.

He slipped it through his arm and said quietly:

"Do not faint here! I think we have had enough dramas for tonight!"

The way he spoke made her give a little chuckle that was half a laugh. Almost at once the carriage was there and he helped her into it.

Only when she could lean against the comfort of the padded back did she shut her eyes and feel as if she was drifting away.

Then Kane was beside her and as they drove off he took her hand in his.

"I should have given you something to drink," he said, "but I will do that as soon as we get home."

His voice seemed to come from afar, and Octavia fought against the darkness that seemed to be closing in on her, thinking it was foolish to be so weak when there was no more danger.

As if Kane knew what she was thinking he said quietly:

"It is all over now and you have been utterly and completely magnificent! How could you have been so clever as to realise what was going on?"

As he spoke the darkness seemed to recede a little and because she longed to explain to him how she had guessed Octavia managed to murmur:

"I . . . I did not tell you before . . . that one of the men who came into my . . . room in Alexandria had a scar under his eye."

"Why did you not tell me?" Kane asked sharply. "I should have noticed it myself."

Because she felt he was rebuking himself because she had been more observant than he had been, again she wanted to laugh.

Then as if he realised how limp she was feeling, he put his arm round her and drew her close to him so that she could rest her head on his shoulder.

"There is no need to talk about it now," he said. "I just want to go on saying how clever you have been to solve a puzzle that has kept everybody in authority guessing from Lord Cromer downwards."

As he finished speaking she knew his lips were on her hair, and she felt the same shafts of moonlight running through her that she had felt when he had kissed her by the Sphinx.

It was so comforting, so perfect to be in his arms, that she did not want to talk.

She just wanted to feel the closeness of him and know that he still loved her even though she was afraid she had lost him.

It was only a short distance from Lord Cromer's house to the Villa, and when they turned in at the gate Octavia remembered that Kane had said they were going home, and she hoped that was what he meant.

She had been so miserable all day thinking he was angry with her that now she wanted to cling not only to him, but to the Villa and never leave either of them.

Then as the horses came to a standstill she told herself she was just dreaming impossible dreams, and she had to be sensible and practical about the future.

Hassam ran down the steps to open the door of the carriage and Kane got down and turned to help Octavia very carefully to the ground.

Then he assisted her up the steps and onto the verandah and having done so said:

"I think as it is very hot you will feel better if you sit for a while in the fresh air. I thought it was very close in the Drawing-Room, but perhaps that was because I was worrying that we should know as little at the end of the evening as we had known at the beginning."

He helped Octavia into one of the comfortable wicker chairs, and comforted her by adding:

"But that was before you brought the whole hideous drama in which we have been engaged for so long to a triumphant conclusion!"

Octavia felt herself thrill at the way in which he spoke.

Then as he lifted her feet carefully onto a stool, he said to Hassam:

"Two brandies, with ice, in long glasses!"

Hassam hurried away and Kane pulled up a chair close to Octavia's and bent forward to take her hand in his.

There was moonlight as there had been last night by the Sphinx, to illuminate the whole garden with silver, and there were also several lanterns hanging along the verandah.

The one above them glittered on the gold of Octavia's hair and made the *diamantés* on her gown twinkle as if the stars had fallen out of the sky and covered her.

Kane looked at her for a long moment before he asked:

"How is it possible that anyone could look so lovely and be so clever? It is a combination I never believed until now could happen."

"It was just...luck," Octavia replied. "If I had not gone back for my bag...Lord Cromer...might have...died."

"That is true," Kane said. "The scorpion was in his bedroom slipper. But tell me how you knew there was a scorpion in his room."

Slowly, finding it hard to find the right words because she still felt so limp, Octavia told him how Lady Cromer had taken the ladies upstairs to her bedroom where they had admired her orchids.

She then explained how when they went downstairs and into the Drawing-Room she realised she had left her bag behind and went back for it.

"The man opened the door next to Lady Cromer's bedroom," she went on, "and seemed very startled at seeing me. I thought it strange that one of the Pasha's servants should be in one of the private rooms of the house."

"It certainly was!" Kane remarked.

"Then as he bowed very low," Octavia went on, "it occurred to me that he was trying to hide his face. He was also pressing something he held in his hands tightly against his chest."

She paused, as if she was trying to think back exactly what had happened, before she continued:

"Then as he scuttled away in a very guilty manner as if he had been doing something wrong, I realised that when I first looked at him I had seen the scar under his eye."

"Why did you not tell me about the scar when you first saw it?" Kane asked.

"I did not think about it," Octavia replied, "and I was not aware until later, after you had killed the other man in the train, not only you but also I was taking part in a Playhouse drama."

Kane laughed.

"It must have seemed like that, my darling! If I had loved you as much when we first met as I do now, I never for one moment would have allowed you to be embroiled in anything so dangerous!"

Because Kane was saying what Octavia wanted to hear, she found it difficult to think of anything but him.

She could feel her love seeping over her so overwhelmingly that all she wanted was that he should kiss her.

Then Hassam arrived with their drinks, and when

Kane handed her a glass Octavia wrinkled her nose and said:

"I would much rather have some fruit juice."

"That you shall have later if you want it," Kane promised, "but think of this as medicine and you can hold your nose while you drink it."

Octavia laughed.

"I will not do that and I will drink it to please you, but I do not like brandy."

"Personally I need a very strong drink!" Kane said. "When I went upstairs after what you had told me, I was praying it might be true and that we had at last caught Abul Pasha after he had evaded us for so long! But I was half-afraid it was something you had imagined."

"I knew you might think that," Octavia replied, "but you were very quick in understanding that I had something to tell you when I asked you for your handkerchief."

"I am not particularly proud of my own reaction," Kane replied. "I have been trained for that, but for you to be so quick-witted and play your part so cleverly is a miracle that I still cannot believe has actually happened."

"But it has . . . and now I need no longer be . . . afraid for . . . you."

Just as Kane was about to answer her there was the sound of a horse's hoofs and they both turned their heads towards the entrance to the Villa.

It was obscured by shrubs and it was therefore a second or so later before round the corner, travelling at some speed, came in sight a horse ridden by a young Officer in uniform.

He pulled up outside the front of the Villa and Kane went down the steps to meet him.

The Officer did not dismount but said in a voice that Octavia could hear quite clearly:

"The Major thought you would wish to know, Sir, that we have found Mr. Manton!"

"Good!" Kane exclaimed. "Was he at Abul Pasha's house?"

"He was locked up in the cellar. We broke down the door and found him there."

"Thank God for that!" Kane exclaimed. "How is he?"

"Weak from lack of food, and of course he has been tortured."

"Badly?"

"Badly enough, but he was, as you can imagine, Sir, very pleased to see us, and the Major has had him taken immediately to the British Hospital where he will be well looked after."

"I am sure of that," Kane said, "and thank you for letting me know."

"The Major told me to come to you at once. He thought you could be home by now, otherwise I was to find you at Lord Cromer's."

"Please thank him," Kane said, "and if you are going back to the Hospital tell them I will call on Mr. Manton first thing tomorrow morning. I think it best for him to be quiet tonight."

"I am sure you are right, Sir. He has been very brave, and he must have had a rotten time!"

The young Officer saluted, turned his horse and rode off.

Octavia knew that Kane gave a deep sigh of relief

before he came up the steps to join her again on the verandah.

As he reached her side he did not sit down but said:

"I am going to take you inside the house because I think you should go to bed. Tonight for the first time for months I shall sleep without worrying about what will happen tomorrow."

Octavia put down her glass and Kane took her hands to pull her to her feet.

Then they went into the hall and as she expected he put his arm round her to help her up the stairs.

Only as she reached the landing did she say:

"I do not want to go to bed. There are so many . . . questions I want to . . . ask you."

"I am thinking of you," Kane answered, "and I think you should rest."

She turned her eyes towards him and he added in a very different tone:

"But if you look at me like that, I shall be unable to let you go!"

Almost without thinking, because his voice evoked such an overwhelming response within her, Octavia walked in through her open bedroom door.

There was a candle alight by her bed, but Hassam had obviously wanted to keep the room cool until her return and the curtains were pulled back.

The windows were wide open so that the moonlight was pouring in to envelop everything with its silver light as brightly as if they were outside in the garden or standing by the Sphinx.

Instinctively Octavia walked across to the window to stand looking up at the stars, remembering how she had prayed for Kane's safety and knowing her prayers had been answered.

Then she felt him come close beside her and realised he had only paused as he crossed the room to pull off his tight-fitting evening-coat with its decorations and throw it down on a chair.

Now he put his arms around her, and as if he was jealous because she was looking at the sky rather than at him, he turned her face round and his lips were on hers.

He kissed her passionately, demandingly, but at the same time she thought, there was something different in his kisses from those he had given her last night.

Now there was something reverent behind the demand of his lips as if perhaps he felt she was very precious.

It was what, alone and miserable, she had wanted and longed for all day.

Now she felt as if the sky had opened and Kane was carrying her up into a special Heaven where they were alone and once again they were part of the moonlight and the music which came from the spheres.

Only when she felt as if the intensity of her feeling was almost too great to be borne, did Octavia with a little murmur turn her head and hide her face against Kane's neck.

Through the fine lawn of his shirt he could feel her trembling against him, and he thought the softness of her and her shyness was the most exciting thing he had ever known.

"I love you, my darling!" he said. "Tell me what you feel about me."

"I love you! You know I . . . love you!"

There was a little tremor in her voice, and it flashed through her mind that perhaps, because he must be aware how overwhelming her love was, he would ask her as he had last night to become his mistress.

She felt she should not have allowed him to come into her bedroom.

Yet at the moment nothing seemed to matter except that he was close to her and his kisses had aroused sensations that were even more glorious and wonderful than they had been before.

Very gently Kane put his fingers under her chin so that he could look down at her again.

Then he said:

"Now all the dragons are vanquished, not by me but by you, my darling, and I can ask you quite simply—how soon will you marry me?"

Octavia's eyes had been half-closed as she had been limp in his arms.

Now he felt her stiffen and her eyes opened wide to look at him before she said:

"Did you . . . did you ask me to . . . m—marry you?"

"I intend to marry you!" Kane said. "And I will not allow you to refuse me!"

There was a smile on his lips as he spoke as if he knew that was impossible.

Octavia made a little sound that was half a laugh and half a sob.

"B—but you said last night that you . . . could not marry me," she managed to say.

"Did you think that was because I did not want you?"

His arms tightened as he went on:

"I want you as I have never wanted anything in the whole world! And nothing, nobody, shall take you from me!"

Octavia felt herself thrill at the possessive, demanding way he spoke, but she still looked at him a little uncertainly, not understanding why he had changed.

As if he understood he said:

"You are the cleverest woman I have ever met, but you are at this moment being very foolish. Surely, my lovely one, you realise that yesterday morning and until half-an-hour ago no sensible person would have insured my life for more than half a *piastre!*"

He pulled her closer to him as he went on:

"How could I marry you, knowing you might be a widow within three minutes of my putting the ring on your finger?"

Octavia gave a murmur of horror and he went on:

"As I have already said, had I loved you as much as I do now, I would have sent you straight back to England instead of involving you in a plot which might, except for your brilliance, have resulted in the death of both Lord Cromer and myself."

He heard her give a cry of fear as she put her arms around his neck.

"I have been frightened, desperately frightened that you would be...killed!" she said. "And all day when you did not come...back I thought you did not...love me any...m-more."

"I love you! You fill the whole world and it is difficult to think of anything except you."

Then he was kissing her, kissing her insistently, demandingly, with a fierceness which told her how

169

much he had been afraid of losing her either through death or because he thought it right to send her away.

Only when their hearts were beating violently against each other's and their breath was coming quickly from between their lips did Octavia hide her face once again in Kane's shoulder.

"I repeat the question I asked you before," he said in a voice that was curiously unsteady. "How soon will you marry me?"

"Now! At this...moment! Tomorrow!" Octavia replied incoherently.

"That is what I want you to say."

"But...you know nothing...about me, and I...think I should...first tell you about myself."

She spoke hesitatingly, wondering if when he knew all about her father he would be shocked.

But she could see in the moonlight that he was smiling as he answered:

"Although I want to know everything about you, my darling, and make sure that in your thoughts and dreams you are all mine, the only thing that matters is that I have found you, and you are the woman I have been looking for all my life."

"Is...that true?"

"You know it is true!" Kane replied. "I have so often been so envious of the Pharaohs, who I always imagine finding great happiness with the lovely women whose heads are painted on their tombs, and thought that I would never feel the same."

"But...what you feel for me...is different?"

"Very, very different," Kane answered. "It is going to take me this life and perhaps several others to tell you how different."

"I am glad...I am so very glad!" Octavia cried.

"At the same time, as I am so ignorant of the world in which you live . . . perhaps you will . . . find me boring."

Kane laughed, and it was a very tender sound.

"Ever since we have known each other, there has been no time for boredom, but only for fear, and now I am going to make sure that we have peace and that our house is full of peace, so that we will always feel safe and secure in it."

His arms tightened as he added:

"I think it would break my heart if ever again I saw you look so afraid as you looked when I first came into your bedroom in Alexandria. And I am aware it was a different fear from what you felt about the men who were trying to kill me."

"That is perceptive of you," Octavia remarked, "because as you know . . . I am afraid of being alone."

"I still cannot understand your brother doing anything so crazy as to leave anyone as beautiful as you are and as I realise now, so young and innocent in a place like Alexandria."

Because the way he said 'innocent' made Octavia remember what he had thought about her, and what he had suggested, she made a little murmur and would have moved away from him if he had not made it impossible.

"You must forgive me," Kane said, knowing there was no need to explain, "but you made me lose my head! I have always prided myself that I could look into the heart of any man or woman whom I was investigating, and know the truth about them."

"H–how . . . could you . . . think such . . . things about me?"

"I can try to excuse myself by saying that it was

171

the circumstances in which I found you, but it was much more than that. I knew before I kissed you that I already loved you overwhelmingly."

He drew close to her and went on:

"But while my heart told me that you were very young and very inexperienced, my worldly mind refused to accept the truth. I wanted you to be mine so desperately that I could think of nothing else."

His lips were against her cheek as he said again:

"Will you forgive me?"

"I love you," Octavia murmured, "and whatever you have . . . done to me . . . or to anybody else, all I want is that you should . . . love me . . . and that I . . . can be your . . . wife."

She spoke the last words very softly and shyly.

And she knew when she felt his heart beating against hers that that was what he wanted to hear.

"We will be married tomorrow, very quietly and very secretly," Kane said.

He knew Octavia wanted to ask him why secrecy was important, and before she could frame the question he explained:

"Everybody tonight, including Lord Cromer, thought we were already married."

"But they must have known that you were using a false name!"

"Actually," Kane replied, "it is my name, and it will be yours."

"You mean . . . you are . . . Lord Stratheagle?"

"I told you I went to England because my father had died, but I was called back here far sooner than I intended."

"Why was that?" Octavia asked.

"First because Manton was missing," Kane answered, "and secondly because I had done a great deal of what one might call espionage work when I was in the Army, and had been called in for several special investigations after I took up what I really most enjoy doing in my life."

"Being an archaeologist."

"Exactly! And I hope it is something you will enjoy too."

Octavia gave a little cry.

"You mean . . . I can come . . . with you?"

"I would not think of leaving you behind! I can assure you, my darling, no discovery I might make, no treasure from any part of the world could be more exciting or more valuable to me than you!"

"It sounds too wonderful to be true!" Octavia exclaimed. "I was afraid that you might only want me to . . . live a social life, and that is . . . something I have no . . . wish to do."

She spoke so positively that Kane looked at her questioningly, and she said:

"You have told me who you are, and it sounds very grand, but . . . please . . . I really want to . . . marry the archaeologist . . . Kane Gordon!"

"That is who you will marry," Kane said, "and it would suit me at any rate, while I am in Egypt to continue to use the name by which I am known to all the people who help me when I am digging, and the ordinary Egyptians who trust me and have nothing to do with men like Abul Pasha."

"I have been . . . praying that I might just be . . . Mrs. Gordon," Octavia said shyly.

"And that is what you will be," Kane smiled, "but

when we go home, as we shall have to do because I have a great many things to see to in Scotland, you will be Lady Stratheagle, and you did say you thought that it was a pretty title."

"A very pretty one!"

Then as if she suddenly remembered she said:

"But I am being...selfish in thinking only of...myself and how much I love you, and there is...something I want you to do for...me."

"What is it, my darling?"

"I want you to try and get in touch with Tony. I feel you are the only person who can do so."

"To tell him about us?"

"No, to tell him what has happened at home!"

The way she spoke made Kane ask quickly:

"What has happened? Something that has upset you?"

"No, no! It is wonderful! But I am afraid when I tell you about it...you will be...shocked at the reason why Tony and I ran away to Alexandria."

"I do not think you could shock me," Kane said gently. "At the same time, as I have already said, I do want to know everything about you."

"It sounds so...wrong now," Octavia said hesitatingly, "but Tony and I felt we would not...stay when Papa died. Tony said there was...nothing we could...do and because Papa owed so much money...it was going to be very...unpleasant..."

"Explain to me first of all," Kane interrupted, "what was your father's name, and where do you live in England?"

"My father was...Lord Birkenhall, perhaps you have...heard of him?"

"Do you mean the Lord Birkenhall who died two weeks or so ago?" Kane asked in surprise.

Octavia nodded, and he said:

"Of course I have met him, and I always thought he was one of the most handsome and charming men I have ever known."

"Many people have said that about . . . Papa."

"He was one of the men I most admired when first I went to London," Kane said. "I was only a young Subaltern and he seemed to represent everything that was smart and dashing. I suppose the fact was that I not only admired, but envied him."

He paused and added:

"But I always thought he was very rich!"

Octavia gave a wry little laugh.

"A lot of people thought that," she said, "but actually Papa was only spending 'dream-money,' and his debts were astronomical. That was why Tony and I ran away."

She thought Kane looked at her in astonishment, and she went on:

"Perhaps . . . it was . . . wrong of us . . . but Papa had neglected the house and the estate, and there was . . . no money except what he spent . . . enjoying himself in London."

The way she spoke told Kane a great deal more than what she said, and after a moment he said very quietly:

"I think your father made you suffer."

Octavia gave a little sob.

"I . . . I cannot explain and you will not . . . understand . . . but it was terrible seeing everything go to . . . rack and ruin . . . and having no money with

which to pay anybody . . . or even have . . . enough for
food!"

She felt Kane draw in his breath, and she said
quickly:

"But now . . . everything is . . . changed!"

"In what way?"

"I know you will think it very . . . reprehensible of
Tony and me that we did not stay for the Funeral . . . but Papa owed such an enormous amount of
money and there was nothing we could do about
it . . . Tony said he would be made bankrupt and everybody would be furious and . . . disagreeable . . . and so
we . . . ran away."

Octavia stopped speaking because she was breathless, and as if she thought Kane did not understand
she looked up at him pleadingly to add:

"Please . . . do not be angry with Tony or . . . me.
I know it was . . . wrong . . . but there was nothing we
could do . . . except watch them raging about the Priory
because there was . . . no money with which to . . . meet
Papa's debts. At least . . . that was what we . . . thought
at the time."

As if she felt she could not explain any more she
moved from the shelter of Kane's arms and went to
the bedside where she had left the newspaper before
dinner.

Picking it up she handed it to him.

"Please read this," she said, "then you will understand why I want to get in touch with Tony and why
I realise now we need not have . . . run away. Now
Tony can pay Papa's debts and not be . . . dependent
for money on marrying some rich girl."

Her words trailed away incoherently.

Kane took the newspaper from her and holding it near the light of the candle read the paragraphs about what had been found at the Priory.

He read it carefully and while he was doing so Octavia watched his face, afraid she might see him looking critical or perhaps even contemptuous because she and her brother had not stayed to face the music.

Then he threw the newspaper down on the floor and put his arms around her again.

"So your brother has his treasure and I have mine," he said, "and, darling, as far as I am concerned, however many pictures and gold frames there are in the world, all I want is to kiss you!"

His lips were seeking hers, but Octavia said:

"Please . . . you will try to find Tony?"

"I will send a cable to him first thing in the morning," Kane promised. "He must go home at once and sort things out but without your help because I need you here! I need you desperately and as I have already said, I will never let you go!"

"And . . . you are not . . . shocked at what we did?"

"I think actually it was very sensible," Kane replied. "If as you thought, there was literally no money with which to meet your father's debts, then there was no point in staying and listening to a lot of abuse which would only have upset you."

His arms tightened around her as he said:

"I will not have you upset, and that is something I shall do my best to prevent for the rest of our lives together."

"You understand . . . oh, Kane, you understand! How can you be so wonderful?"

"Of course I understand, my precious, and before

177

you worry any more about your brother or any other relatives you may have, I want you to look after your husband and take care of him, as you have done already, but in a rather different way."

"I thought you were going to take care of me!" Octavia teased.

"You can be quite certain I shall do that," Kane replied, "and as we have a great deal to learn about each other, the moment we are married tomorrow— as I have already said, it will be a secret marriage which nobody will know about except the Parson who is a great friend of mine and will perform the ceremony—we will set off on our honeymoon."

"Our . . . honeymoon?"

"I saw a friend in London," Kane explained, "who told me that when I returned to Egypt I could borrow his private steam-yacht. I think, my darling, you will find it a very enjoyable way of spending our honeymoon, to travel up the Nile to Luxor."

Octavia's eyes were shining like stars.

"Can we . . . really do that?" she asked. "I have longed to see the Nile and to be on it alone with you would be very . . . very exciting!"

"That is what I thought," Kane said, "and that is what we will do, my precious one. But I am afraid the rest of your trousseau will have to wait until we return to Cairo."

"But . . . I have so much . . . already, and I want to show it to you."

"And I want to see it," Kane said tenderly, "but what I really want is to hold you in my arms, to make love to you, on what to the Pharaohs was the 'River of Life,' and also—the River of Love!"

Then he was kissing Octavia, kissing her possessively, demandingly, as if she was already his.

As she felt her whole being respond and as she quivered against him he knew they were one person and nothing would ever divide them.

His kisses became more passionate and she hid her face.

"I am . . . frightened," she whispered.

"But why, my darling?" Kane asked. "There is nothing to frighten you here."

She did not speak and after a moment he asked:

"You are not frightened of—me?"

"Not of . . . you but the . . . way you make me . . . feel."

"How do I make you feel?"

His voice was very gentle and quiet.

"It was when you . . . kissed me . . . by the . . . Sphinx!"

"What happened?"

"The moonlight . . . seemed to shine . . . into my body . . . and run . . . through me . . . it was very . . . wonderful . . . but . . ."

Octavia's voice died away.

"What happened—then?"

"I felt you carried me up . . . to the Stars and . . . it was so . . . marvellous . . . there are no . . . words to describe . . . it."

"But now you are frightened?"

"Only because the moonlight is still there . . . but now it is . . . like little . . . flames of . . . fire."

"And they frighten you?"

"They make . . . me feel . . . very . . . very excited . . . and sort of wild . . . is that . . . wrong?"

Kane gave a little laugh which was caught in his throat and his eyes were very tender.

"No, my precious—my innocent darling, it is right—absolutely right."

"You are . . . sure?"

"Absolutely sure—and when we are married I will make you understand that what you are feeling is love—the real love which every man seeks but is afraid he will never find."

"I love . . . you . . . I . . . love you."

"Not half as much as I will make you love me."

There was silence before Octavia said:

"I did not . . . know that love was like . . . moonlight and . . . fire."

"It is all that and so much more."

"Perhaps . . . that is the real . . . meaning of . . . the Sphinx."

"But of course it is, the mystery, the enigma, and the eternity of love which we all have to find for ourselves."

"Have I found . . . it?"

"I hope so . . . my lovely one and I will teach you to love me with moonlight and fire until you burn with the glory of it as I am burning now."

"Teach me! Oh . . . please teach me!"

Kane's lips were on hers and the shafts of moonlight running through her turned to flames and fused with the fire which was raging in him.

Then Octavia knew his love for her was not only the love of a man for a woman, but was part of the spiritual ecstasy that belonged to the mystery of the Sphinx, and the glory of the ancient gods.

It was around them and a part of them.

Because they were aware of it, she knew it would make their marriage a voyage which would extend into the eternal life in which there is no death.

As Kane's kisses swept her up to the stars she whispered:

"I love you . . . I love . . . you."

"I worship you."

Then there was only the moonlight turning to fire and the love which continues ever and always into Eternity.

ABOUT THE AUTHOR

Barbara Cartland, the world's most famous romantic novelist, who is also an historian, playwright, lecturer, political speaker and television personality, has now written over 370 books and sold over 370 million books the world over.

She has also had many historical works published and has written four autobiographies as well as the biographies of her mother and that of her brother, Ronald Cartland, who was the first Member of Parliament to be killed in the last war. This book has a preface by Sir Winston Churchill and has just been republished with an introduction by Sir Arthur Bryant.

Love at the Helm, a novel written with the help and inspiration of the late Admiral of the Fleet, the Earl Mountbatten of Burma, is being sold for the Mountbatten Memorial Trust.

Miss Cartland in 1978 sang an Album of Love Songs with the Royal Philharmonic Orchestra.

In 1976 by writing twenty-one books, she broke the world record and has continued for the following seven years with twenty-four, twenty, twenty-three, twenty-four, twenty-four, twenty-five, and twenty-three. She is in the *Guinness Book of Records* as the best-selling author in the world.

She is unique in that she was one and two in the Dalton List of Best Sellers, and one week had four books in the top twenty.

In private life Barbara Cartland, who is a Dame of the Order of St. John of Jerusalem, Chairman of the St. John Council in Hertfordshire and Deputy President of the St. John Ambulance Brigade, has also fought for better conditions and salaries for Midwives and Nurses.

Barbara Cartland is deeply interested in Vitamin Therapy and is President of the British National Association for Health. Her book *The Magic of Honey* has sold throughout the world and is translated into many languages. Her designs "Decorating with Love" are being sold all over the U.S.A., and the National Home Fashions League named her in 1981, "Woman of Achievement."

Barbara Cartland's Romances (a book of cartoons) has recently been published in Great Britain and the U.S.A., as well as *Getting Older, Growing Younger*, and a cookery book, *The Romance of Food*.

BARBARA CARTLAND

CAMFIELD NOVELS OF LOVE